T0208092

Time Heals All Wounds

Time Heals All Wounds

Jon Chris

iUniverse®

TIME HEALS ALL WOUNDS

iUniverse books may be ordered through booksellers or by contacting:

iUniverse
1663 Liberty Drive
Bloomington, IN 47403
www.iuniverse.com
1-800-Authors (1-800-288-4677)

ISBN: 978-1-4917-8050-3 (sc)
ISBN: 978-1-4917-8051-0 (e)

Library of Congress Control Number: 2015917714

Print information available on the last page.

iUniverse rev. date: 11/18/2015

For Guy R. Jones

Chapter 1

"I have no clue as to why you don't listen to me, I'm telling you this because I love you. Your little friends who you think are your friends don't care anything about you – can't you see that? When you get caught up in those streets you will probably be the fall guy – wake up!"

Ms. LaShaun Denise Holloway or better known as Shaun, my girl. She loved to tell me off every now and then and I deserved it at times but one thing that we do know besides all the nagging is that she loves my black ass to death! We lived in a sumptuous apartment complex way out west with the middle class folks in Eagle Creek. She's twenty-three and I'm twenty-one. She is ten credits away from earning her Bachelors in Child Psychology which she works on at nights at Butler. By day she handles clerical work at a prestige OBGYN office in downtown. She drove a 1999 ES-300 that her father bought her on her twenty-first birthday which is how we met …

I called myself practicing driver safety one afternoon while paused at a red light near the motor Speedway and started to fidget with the earpiece to my cell, it fell down towards my foot and I reached for it. Somehow my foot eased off the brake and by then it was too late. I had fender- bended into a Lexus! I hesitated on fleeing the scene; no insurance and my license were suspended – my ass was in some trouble but what exited the car made me put my Electra in park. I cancelled all thoughts on fleeing because this girl was worth going to jail for a few nights. She wasn't only a goddess but a sweet concerned goddess who was more worried about my safety as to her own. She stood around 5'2 and looked to weigh about 130 pounds; her skin was a flawless cinnamon complexion, her eyes were a dark honey tone and the baby blue scrubs that she wore proved that her breast and butt were perfect – not too little and not too big. I loved long hair on a woman but she wore hers short, but I still thought she was gorgeous. I was whipped but yet I hadn't even spoken to this perfect little thing but since that fender bender Shaun and I found ourselves inseparable.

"Shaun, calm your nerves. I got this. There's no need to spit venom on Juan or anyone I kick it with, Juan would be the first one there to post my bond with a top-notch lawyer if the time ever comes."

"Are you crazy? What honestly makes you believe that? He's the worse one; I can see right through his fakeness." Her chest heaved as she snatched her purse off of the kitchen counter. "I can't believe you right now, you seriously think –"

"Can we end this conversation please, you don't …"

"I don't what?" She kept it going while brushing past me in search of something.

"Look! Look at this!" I had reached into my pocket. "We're doing fine; we got plenty of money, we're sucka free and we're the truth!"

"Boy, you're crazy. That's the truth. Where is my …"

"You're phone is on top of your purse."

"Thank you. Javon, baby, that money that you're flashing won't do you any bit of good when you're in jail or dead."

"Gotdamn! Who said anything about either one – don't wish that shit on me!" I forced my money back into my jeans.

"I'm not wishing it on you, you're flirting with it."

"Will you stop! All you do is talk shit."

"I'll stop talking shit when you start to act like you have some sense and leave those damn streets alone." She cut her honey brown eyes at me. "I love you Javon but your ways, I hate. And the company that you keep, I despise." She stared deep into my dark browns that read annoyance.

"How come you never complain when it's time to go shopping in Chicago, Edinburg and all your other little fancy shopping spots or when it's rent time?"

"Excuse me but do you honestly think that I need your money?"

"No but –"

"Stop, let me answer that. Have you forgotten how much legal money I make; I can buy my own clothing, boots, heels, panty and bras, and our rent. If you didn't have a dime I'd still love you without a doubt."

"If I was broke you'd still love me? Yeah right! No female wants a broke ass dude – shut your spoiled ass up girl, if my parents owned their own business then –"

"My parents don't give me a damn thing!" Her voice shot up a few octaves.

"Right."

"Javon, I work hard for mine and I know how to save."

"I work hard for mine too."

"I wish that you could hear how stupid you sound right now. I'm talking about an honest living; if you call what you do honest then you've got another thing coming."

I sat quietly for a moment while her words pierced through me.

She calmed her nerves and said: "I told you a long time ago that my daddy would give you a job – shoot, you sell drugs so well that I don't see why you'd have a hard time selling cars."

"I don't need any handouts Shaun."

"It's not a handout." She spoke with her hands.

"Then what is it?"

"It's a job, a good one at that. I'm trying to guide you in the right – you know what forget it. My mother always told me that you can't help someone who doesn't want help."

Good, now shut the fuck up I thought while we stood in silence for what seemed like a decade.

"I'm going to stop past my mother's office and then I'm off to gym, you want to come? I think they're playing ball tonight."

"Nawh, I'm cool. Need to finish putting that tree together." I pointed to an artificial Christmas tree.

"You should've bought a real one."

I nodded my head while she grabbed her gym bag, she'd then come back to stand in front of me. She tried to kiss me.

"Give me a kiss boy." She dropped her bag and leaped onto me making us fall backwards into the couch.

"Get off of me crazy ass girl."

She laughed before biting my cheek then kissed me. Her lips were beyond soft and full, matter of fact; they always reminded me of Megan Goods.

"Aight now, don't start anything that you can't finish." I whispered.

"You started this."

I noticed her nipples coming to life through her gray halter which forced me to kiss the top of her chest, I picked her up, moved her to pin her between the door and wall. I caressed her stomach and oddly felt her firmness disappear a bit. My hand found its way underneath her sports bra to massage her breast. *Damn, did they get bigger?* I thought. I pulled her top up enough to let her perfect natural C cups fall out into gravity and she'd tense as I licked around her dark areolas. She'd moan lightly while her hand found its way down to my zipper and with ease she was stroking more than my ego. My left hand palmed her lower arch while my right tugged at her stretch pants, she gracefully stepped one leg out at a time panties included. I started to explore through her femininity and she'd squirm and sigh as I teased her more than usual wetness. I had to pause and view my hand – my finger displayed pure liquid! "You okay?" I whispered.

"I'm fine – don't stop … thsss"

"Guess we should argue more often."

With that being said she took control of me and guided my penis into her with such ease. I had never been able to enter her like that. Something was different about her, but, things continued. After only four minutes of our fiesta she bit down on her bottom lip, her eyes rolled and she bucked forcefully while I had her braced against the wall. Her nails found a new home in my back, her grip was painful and uncalled for, she screamed in passion, and slowly but surely stopped.

"What's wrong?" I questioned in disbelief.

She abruptly pulled me out of her and pulled her top back down, "You aren't about to have me all wore out and tired before my workout."

"What? You used me! You got a quick nut off and now you want to leave me – how dare you!"

She was by then in our room laughing her soul out, "Boy, I didn't even come so what are you talking about." She came back out with a smirk painted on her face.

"Oh, you didn't! Well can you explain this then?" I pointed to my penis.

"Okay, and so what if I did – like you've never done it before."

She had a point. I was looking crazy as hell lost for words and stuck with a hard wet dick. She grabbed her coat and bag attempting to get by me.

"Put your sha bong bong up."

"No. You put it up, you took it out!"

She tried for the door again with a devilish grin and said, "Be ready for round two when I get back."

Shaun complained quite a bit but I imagine that she did it out of love for me, we had been together for almost two years and the girl had a huge impact on my life. She helped me grow into a man kind of fast. Some things came natural and by instinct for a man while others needed guidance, skill, perfection and schooling. This is where she helped me. She was a church girl, the type that goes to service every Sunday, reads the announcements, goes to Wednesday night bible studies and participates in quite a few church functions. But … we all know about the church girls; as soon as service was over the word sin was erased from their mental rolodex to an extent. She lived life on the edge and was filled with spontaneous energy, well; at least she did in the beginning. Our sex life was great at first but soon the freak turned to an insert tab A into slot B kind of girl. Boring.

She couldn't stand the fact that I was more than some part-time petty hustler but she knew about this early on, I guess she figured that she would be able to change me but of course it wouldn't be that simple. Or would it? Little did she know I had just avoided telling her the news that would have scarred her for life. I didn't tell her, not that night at least.

CHAPTER 2

Time was flying by rapidly. So rapidly that I couldn't even count the days. Her breasts were getting fuller, her stomach lost its firmness and her sex was different all for a reason. Her moods were flip flop and her eating was even a little odd. Three months had passed since that night and unbeknownst of me she was already three months pregnant then, so, that meant I'd be a proud father to a little angel. A baby girl.

During those months I had critical thoughts and tough decisions to decide on. I had to get my act together because I had a huge responsibility coming my way and regardless of my age I'd handle it. I wanted to go back to working an honest living but the drug money was like a drug within itself – addictive. Dope fiends were addicted to crack while I and a million others were addicted to fast money. I had to do some serious soul searching because choices needed to be made.

She called it right on the nose. The streets swallowed me alive.

She posted four grand for my forty thousand dollar bond or actually I paid for it she just had access to a little bit of my money. You can never be too careful in the streets; timing, knowledge and luck has a huge say so in a hustler's life. My knowledge was on point but my timing and luck sure as hell wasn't. I was charged with two class A felonies, a dealing in cocaine charge and a possession which in Indiana is similar to life sentences if found guilty and that's if you don't cop out to a plea or help the authorities make their job a little easier. I wouldn't take a plea nor would I snitch.

I'll never forget the demeanor that her pregnant body read; she was disgusted, pissed, embarrassed and most of all … hurt. I was disgusted with myself – this is what the fuck I deserved. I can remember being in the county jail still and I had to have my sister relay the news to my grandmother, I couldn't tell her, what was I supposed to say *Grandma, I know you'd buy me anything but I'd rather sell crack.* And then my mother, she was probably cussing me out right from heavens entrance. Shaun's mother saw me on the eleven o'clock news while her father read the front page of the Indianapolis News: *I.P.D. Sweep Northeast Side Drug Dealers.* Under the bold print was a portrait of Juan and me looking as if we had just caught a deadly virus – we did. The system.

So much was going on and so fast. My mind wasn't cooperating and my nerves were bad so how was I supposed to ease the stress? Couldn't smoke any chronic, couldn't pop any ecstasy – couldn't give the court any reason to revoke my bond before trial. I'd end up boosting my drinking up; Bombay, Vox, and grey goose – goose … how could I forget. That was our drink. She'll never speak to me again, I flooded her with lie after lie. I was in pain when it came to her … *I'm sorry baby girl, so sorry.*

May 2002

My grandmother and sister sat in the front row on a dark oak bench that had pain, suffering, anger and probably even a bit of joy and relief soiled in it. To their right stood the solid blue state flag and above it read a pledge: *IN GOD WE TRUST.* In the center of the room stood a raven chair behind a large credenza and behind it read *SUPERIOR COURT #20.* My attorney sat next to me looking like anything but ready for trial but yet the blond prosecutor who resembled a broke down version of Sharon Stone sat across from us looking prepared for war. My ace, my brother from another mother, my co-defendant Juan Wilkes entered the court-room. I hadn't really seen him due to all this bull shit. I became confused when I saw that he wasn't wearing a suit, he was in street attire when he and his attorney passed by us with no eye contact. For a split second my eyes deceived – no they didn't. I blinked when Juan and his attorney stopped in front of Sharon Stones table to whisper, she grinned then nodded in agreement – I was officially in a world of trouble after that. I was in a serious zone until I scanned the court-room, I could have sworn that I saw her in the very back of the court-room. It wasn't her.

Time went by like lightning and all I could remember was fumbling through the inside of my suit jacket to read my phone *6lbs 12in She looks like u* I blinked my tear away as I noticed the same group of twelve people from earlier returning to their assigned seats. My timing and luck wasn't shit, never had been. As my child was being brought into the world, her father, Javon C. Hardman was being taken out of it.

CHAPTER 3

Some say that life is like a deck of cards being that today you may get dealt a good hand but tomorrow you might get dealt a terrible hand. Others say that life can be compared to chess because you have to know how to maneuver your players in order to keep them from falling captive and yet still checkmate your opponent which is similar to life. But I wonder what would happen if a person got dealt a bad hand for what seemed like a lifetime or what if a person made all the wrong moves during chess? You'd think that one should consider stopping with the card games or learning how to play the cards that are dealt and I'd imagine that you would have to watch the chess board a lot closer to prevent capture in order to win.

I became a descent chess player when I entered L3CF. It was located right underneath Michigan but still within Indiana border lines in a small town called Bunker Hill which was Hicksville to the heart. The prison was huge and by it being connected to an air force base only made it look bigger. Prison wasn't exactly how society, the media or the movies made it out to be; no one ever dropped the soap and if they did nothing would get plugged up their ass. Gays did exist in there but they associated with their own kinds which were *homo-thugs* or their *sistas.* To a majority of us the hardest part about being locked up was the fact of being stripped away from family and friends while at the same time our freedom and rights have been revoked, this alone was enough to disturb a person mentally, emotionally and physically.

I began to dislike everyone; the judge, prosecutor, my drunk ass attorney, Juan's bitch ass and anyone else who had anything to do with me getting sent to a living hell including myself. I cried many nights at first because I felt sorry for myself. I could've understood a lighter sentence especially with my non-criminal history but yet they treated me like I had murdered someone – maybe I – never mind. Of course I couldn't forget that I didn't cooperate with them either, had I snitched then my sentence wouldn't have been so harsh but I wouldn't dare bring another man or team down with me due to my own carelessness – don't know how many would agree with me in this day and age. But again, this was Indiana, a state with the most up and running prisons, a state that makes laws up as they go (Johnnie Cochran's exact words) and the state that hands out the most time for non-violent crimes. Even Ray Charles, Mike Tyson, Isaiah Thomas and numerous famous folks will warn you about visiting Indiana.

After three months into my thirty year sentence (serve fifteen years) my spirit changed one Friday morning. That was my first visitation. That was my first time seeing my baby in real life. I held her and if that little bundle of joy wasn't an exact clone of myself then the devil was a lie. She had her mother's skin and grade of hair but her facials features were all mine right down to the dimple in our chins. I could taste the bitterness and pain seeping from Shaun's pores during our visit but I couldn't do anything besides enjoy the time with my creation. She wouldn't be mad at me forever; I believed that this time would heal her and me.

I kissed my baby on her plump cheeks and she cooed with a smile, I'd gnaw on her tiny fingers and she absolutely loved that. I held her high in the air while she drooled on me, an invisible tear rolled down my eye as I whispered to her *daddy loves you baby, daddy will be home soon, I promise.*

I didn't think that Shaun was going to stick by my side like she did. She held me down during the early stages by keeping money on my books regardless if it were hers or mine. A block never came on her phone while she made it a priority to keep me uplifted with cards, pictures and letters. She'd let our apartment go and move in with her parents to help out with the baby, I thanked God for all of them every night – when I wasn't upset with Him. The hardest part with Shaun was telling her that she needed to move on with her life. I didn't want her waiting on me for no amount of time because I realized early on that she was still a woman and women had numerous needs that needed full attention and obviously I couldn't provide any of them. I wanted her to live her life but yet keep my daughters in mine. If she got with another brother then all I could ask from him was for her to be well taken of and for my seed to be loved like how he would love his own. This was my reality which was a hard pill to swallow but it was either that or go insane over something I had no control over.

CHAPTER 4

At the age of twelve I was able to witness the best of both worlds.

My mother, Phylicia Hardman raised my younger sister and I alone. We lived north of downtown in a two bedroom duplex on a street where drugs, murder and prostitution lingered heavily, however, my mother still held us together. She made too much money to receive welfare and even if she didn't make enough she was so stubborn to where she wouldn't accept any help especially from the state. She still got us by with the grace of God and class. But when she died in the car accident we had to live with our grandmother who lived out north in the suburbs. Mrs. Jane Hardman whom we called *moma* was an angel in the flesh. My mother and her shared very similar characteristics when it came to genes but their attitudes and priorities were on another level. The move to moma's wasn't that bad, I got adjusted to the township schools with the quickness because that was one thing that she did not play with – education. She enforced that rule to the fullest; not only was she a retired math and social studies teacher but she made her kids go to college. She told me that I'd be on the first thing smoking to Indiana University as soon as I graduated from high school but she had no clue that I was on another agenda. She also pushed employment on me at the age of fourteen, my work permit was signed and ready to go! My grandmother was my mother, father and best friend all in one – I loved her to no limit.

Chapter 5

They say that prison can preserve the body and its features if one was willing to take care of themselves. I looked the same in my eyes; I sure as hell wasn't growing any taller but I had to admit that being 5'7 had its up's and down's though. My skin was a sandy brown during the winter but when summer rolled around it would turn dark brown and my one hundred and eighty pound build was healthy but the weights toned it up a bit. I wore my hair low enough to witness an ocean of waves while my eyes did the same as my skin.

I stayed to myself a majority of the time while I was away. I associated with one brother who knew of me through my close friend Ricky. Marcus was his name and he was a stand up kind of guy, he was grimy when needed to be but overall he was a good brother. He was doing time on a drug case as well. So we'd partner up on the spade table, play chess and go hard on the dominoes but I still didn't want to be too close with another man after what Juan had done to me – I couldn't believe that he got up there and testified against me!

In prison, every day was exactly the same. Same people, same clothing, same nasty ass food and the same routines. The only thing that didn't stay the same was the clock but this was a good thing.

Many nights as I would lay on the metal bunk I'd do mass thinking; some of my thoughts were future, some were present but a majority of them were past thoughts. Thinking in the past had its advantages and disadvantages. The advantages helped ease my pain and mind especially when I thought about the good times that I had with the fellas at the clubs, strip clubs; the cars, the money but most of all my relationship with her. The disadvantages caused a negative reaction because I'd find myself thinking about all of the people who I had done wrong to knowing that they didn't deserve it. I sold crack to mothers, fathers, aunts, uncles, grandparents and so on; these people's lives were probably already devastated and on the verge of destruction but yet I was feeding them poison. I ruined children's chances of getting new school clothes, latest toy, or probably even food because their parent chose to spend their last eighty dollars on a gram or so. Not to mention the pain and lost that I caused towards my own family and friends. But … I imagined that it was way too late to be fretting over what I couldn't change …

***

December 1998

Snow was on the ground, not heavy but enough to drive semi cautiously. It was a serious drought on dope throughout the city and Ricky, Juan and I were broker than broke. Neither one of us had a dime saved and yet Christmas was around the corner. I had a job making close to nine dollars an hour but that wasn't any money and plus I was on the verge of being fired any damn way. I was broke. I was so broke that my cousin Sinobia called my phone this night in particular offering gas money to take her to her friend's place. Sinobia

Hardman was my first cousin; she was my Uncle Lee's only child and had me by two years in age. She was a true red bone like the rest of the women in my family but the only thing about her was the fact that she had a slight money fetish. I loved her to death and would've never charged her for anything let alone for a ride but it just so happened that I was several blocks away from her apartment on the west side and my gas needle was flirting with the other side of the E. I can remember how she was bragging about the guy on the journey to his place; she said that he had money out the ass and then some. I took heed to what she was saying but any other time I would've crossed examined her about the man's money being her only interest. I had other intentions this go 'round. I let her continue on as she pointed to his apartment from the highway. We pulled into the complex and the first thing that caught my eye was a dark-colored Lexus parked in the front. I made sure that she got in safe as I discreetly memorized the door she knocked on.

After several nights of investigating the boys and I saw what we wanted and went for it. My heart switch was off while my mind was poisoned with embalming fluid along with B.G.'s influential lyrics from *Dangerous Grounds*, both of these equaled out a strong adrenaline rush.

"Ya'll ready?" I questioned

With luck the door went through with one kick from Juan, the man was just about sleep before we invaded his privacy; he was stretched out on his beige Corinthian leather.

"Merry Christmas nigga!" I smacked him across the head with my gun. "Get ya ass on the floor and don't fuckin move!"

"Man, he has some tight ass leathers: Pelle, Davouchi, Phat –"

"Fuck those coats – find the money while I tie him up. I think I hit him too hard." I told Juan.

"You could have made this a lot easier J; we could've made him tell us where the shit was." Ricky said in aggravation.

"Too late for that shit cause he is out cold – let's go treasure huntin."

The man's place was lavish as hell. He owned high-end furniture and his entertainment system was top of the line. He also owned several paintings that looked expensive; one in particular that caught my attention seemed to be an illusion of a figure falling backwards into a never-ending vortex, I thought it was the drugs messing with my mind but I guess I'll never know. We tore that place apart; every shoe box was thrown out onto the floor, every piece of luggage was thrown, mattress – tossed, cabinets and drawers – yanked out. A robbery should never take that long, we spent too much damn time in there and to make matters worse we didn't find a damn dime. I was pissed off about the whole thing. I snatched my mask off and stormed out the back exit empty-handed while my crew had bags filled with the man's possessions. I nodded my head in anger and humility at them before sliding into the backseat of the 94 Road master. The wet stick, which I rarely smoked, was playing major tricks with my mind because I couldn't manage to see anything besides a human figure falling into a dark vortex. I snapped out of it when Ricky forced the power steering to screech.

"Whoa bruh, watch the car over here." I warned him. But suddenly I saw that the car we almost hit was that Lexus, "Did ya'll see any keys in there?"

Juan looked back at me like I was a damn fool, "Might've been a pair on that glass table – why?"

"Stop the car!"

"Wassup man?" Ricky punched the brake.

"I gotta see something real quick." I snatched my gun and mask before dashing back up to the apartment. Rich boy was still out cold, breathing but out for the count. I saw what I wanted and grabbed them, my heart skipped a beat when I witnessed the *L* symbol on one of the keys, I smiled to myself and began to make a move until I saw something. My mind was still cloudy but I could not have been hallucinating when I saw a figure in the doorway blocking my exit. Figured it was Juan at first with his slender and tall build but I soon found out that this figure had a gun pointed at me. I studied this all black figure a second too long because the next thing I knew I heard a light but powerful gust of wind that forced me backwards into the glass table. It shattered into a billion pieces and before I could reach for my trigger another gust of wind flew past me. I pulled my trigger and nearly awoke the dead; I rolled over and studied the doorway. No one or nothing was there. Couldn't understand what was happening to me. I leaped up cautiously toward the door and looked to my left; Juan and Ricky were sprinting towards me with their guns drawn. I looked towards my right but nothing was there besides the empty front steps. My heart rate picked up *what the fuck* I thought.

"What the fuck?" Juan looked over me studying Rich boy, "You didn't shoot him did you?"

"Hell nawh – ya'll see anybody in the hallway?"

"Boy you trippin' – come on we gotta go. Now! Who the hell were you shooting at?" Ricky led us out.

"Somebody shot at me, I think." I explained before stopping at the Lexus. By then my heart-felt like it was going to beat its way through my chest and my head was throbbing like crazy but I still managed to press the key to see if it was a match. It was a match! I checked under the seats and then the glove compartment, nothing was there but I still popped the trunk. As I moved I felt a sharp pain shoot through my shoulder, I could hear Juan rushing me as I continued to maneuver through the trunk. I noticed an amp, a set of speakers, two foot locker bags and a duffle bag wedged behind the speakers.

I grabbed all the bags, dove into the car and that was about all that I could remember prior to seeing blood on my hands and a dark twister vortex that I was falling into.

CHAPTER 6

I was awakened by a woman hollering. A holler mixed with a painful moan. I sat up in an unfamiliar bed with sudden pain in my shoulder. I glanced around the hospital type room and noticed my clothing sitting on a trash bag on top of what looked like a baby changing station. *Where am I?* I wondered.

I was in the midst of getting out the bed when I felt more crucial pain coming from my shoulder, I touched it and realized that I was bandaged. *What the fuck.* I eased my jeans on with my good arm and started to investigate the place a little more but suddenly the lady hollered again but this time it had timely breathing patterns accompanied with it. I stuck my head into the hallway to follow the hollering which led to an adjacent room from the one I was in; I chose to be noisy by peeping through the cracked door and witnessed three women bringing a baby into this cruel world.

"Push honey, push … good. Now breathe. I can see his head crowning now." That was the middle-aged white lady who seemed to have control over everything. "You're doing fine honey. Give me one small push and relax for a moment."

It was silent for exactly one minute until she yelped again and scaring me, I bumped my head on the door and they all looked at me in unison. The white lady waved me in a hurry.

"We need your help. I need you to come hold her hand."

The woman in labor shot me a look that said *hurry your ass up!* And as ironic as this was I went around to the girl and gave her my good arm and within a split second I could have sworn that she was trying to arm wrestle me.

"Doctor, she's dilating again." That was the pleasantly plump lady who was assisting.

"Alright baby, give me a good long one."

I had no idea who the hell this girl was which made me wonder where the hell her child's father was; why wasn't he there holding her hand and did this girl care that I could practically see her entire body! Her full breast bounced out of her gown with every jerk while her legs were spread beyond eagle displaying every single fold, crease and crevice of her womanhood.

"Is my baby coming?" She asked me in haste.

"Hunh? I-I don't know."

She about broke my hand with her delicate fingers, "Look and see!" She lost all focus on the doctors and placed it on me.

"Uh, excuse me but is her –"

She pulled my arm damn near out of its socket and spoke violently, "I told you to look and see!" She put the fear of God in me.

I looked down between her legs and saw quite a bit; saw the top of a small hairy head begging to come out of her. This was my first time seeing a baby born and it messed me up a little to see how wide she had opened up and it made me think twice about what a damn penis could do to a vagina if it expanded like that. Six minutes later the clock on the wall read 11:51 a.m. and a healthy baby boy with perfect vocals had just entered the world.

"Oh! Twins! She's having another baby!" I yelled after seeing something else exiting her.

"Relax baby, it's only after birth." The plump lady said.

After witnessing the afterbirth pour out of her, I stormed out of that damn room. Watching a baby come was one thing but the other mess was another.

It was probably twenty minutes later when the heavy-set lady introduced herself as Debra, Ricky's Aunt. She explained how Ricky had called her close to midnight the night before explaining that I'd been shot and wasn't responding. He told her that a hospital would not have been the best idea, I guess she obviously knew what he meant by that and forced them to bring me to her job ASAP. She told them that I'd be fine that I'd be fine since the bullet went in and out but I did lose a little bit of blood. I thanked her sincerely while questioning her about repaying her.

"Honey, you've repaid me already. You helped that young lady bring her first baby into the world, you coached her."

"That's called coaching?" She laughed at my sarcasm as I thought about the girl turning into an evil demon.

"I do have a question though."

"Ask away."

"What exactly is this place?"

"This is what they call a mid-wife clinic." She answered proudly. "Dr. Klein and I have had our license for almost ten years now."

"What did Dr. Klein say about me?"

"Well, let's just say that this isn't our first rodeo." She pointed to my shoulder as I heard faint baby cries coming from the other room.

"What did she name her son?"

"Why don't you go in there and find out, she was wondering if you were ok after the way you ran out the room."

"Is she done with all that extra stuff coming out of her?"

"What the afterbirth – child yes." She giggled at me before I made my way to the other room.

I walked in right as the newborn was being fed which made me ease back out with an apology.

"Hey." She yelled softly.

I put my head to the door, "Are you two doing okay?"

"Come on in, I don't think that breast-feeding will scare you, will it?"

For some odd reason the girl looked a lot different from when she was in labor. She was a cutie. She looked like she had a pinch of foreign to her but her black roots dominated. Her voice was so soft and comforting, she spoke with mannerism and she looked to be in her early twenties as well. I glanced at her son and accidentally caught a glimpse of a full dark nipple.

"You're going to have problems with little girls calling your home because he's going to be a heartbreaker. What's his name?"

"I know, thank you. His name is Christopher Miguel Williams." She announced proudly.

"That's a nice strong name, is he a junior?"

"No!"

"My fault." I raised my hands in the air catching a horrific pain in my shoulder. "What's your name again?" I changed my tempo in a rush.

"Zanada. Zanada Williams." She extended her small hand. I did the same only to catch another agonizing pain.

"Shit." I shook her soft hand lightly, "That's a pretty name, zuh-nod-uh, unique too."

"Thank you – are you okay?"

"I'm fine, it's just a scratch, thankyou though."

"A scratch, yeah right – a gunshot is far from a scratch."

"Guess you're right but I'm fine, I'm a big boy."

"Oh so now you're a big boy? I couldn't tell when you ran out of here not too long ago."

"That's different. That was some nasty shit."

"No its not. It's part of the process, you don't have any kids?"

"No, not yet."

"Oh. Well, at least when you do you will now be prepared." She giggled while shifting her son. "Thank you for being here for me, after all; I am a complete stranger and here I was cussing you out while coming close to having your hand amputated."

"It's cool, glad that I could help. Guess I got ... *scratched* for a reason." I grinned. "Well, Ms. Zanada; I must go, I have some business to attend to but it was nice to meet you considering these unusual circumstances. Take care of this little fellow, he's a gift." I was on my way out her room until she said:

"You never told me your name."

"I'm sorry, it's Javon ... Javon Hardman."

"Well nice meeting you too Javon considering these unusual circumstances. Try to be a little more careful out there."

CHAPTER 7

After speaking with Ricky and Juan later that afternoon I felt a sense of relief even though the last twenty-four hours of my life had been unreal. It was obvious that the drugs weren't the only issue when it came to my mental state that night because there was definitely someone in that doorway and whoever it was shot me. I'll never know who, what or why they were there but my only guess was that the same person had come to pay rich boy a visit as well – we just beat them to the punch. What in the hell were the chances of getting shot, then rescued by an obstetrician and yet help out with a baby's birth all within twenty-four hours! Only in someone's wild novel would you hear of such a thing.

The good news was that the Lexus was indeed the jackpot. The gym bag held a significant amount of money – close to $50,000 and the shoe boxes inside the footlocker bags held nearly 4 bricks of dope. How I knew to check the trunk I'll never know, maybe a hustler's instinct – I'll never know. I took a bullet behind that shit but I guess it was a bullet of investment. We split everything down the middle except for me and my injury pension – I took two of the bricks. Everybody was satisfied for the moment. Christmas that year ended up being a huge success but we took a vow to let the dope sit until after the New Year; a tradition that was rarely followed by dope boys in the game.

After the New Year we took our product and demolished the North East side, North West, and lower East side apart! Jumping from a packman to a birdman was amazing within itself. Our supplier became this "Bonnie and Clyde" type couple who were neither Columbian, Mexican nor Middle Eastern – they were American. Maybe their connect was across the water or border but we didn't give a damn as long as we were stocked with a good product. Phatima and Porsha loved us because we were one of their best customers if not *the* best, but yet, we never asked any questions about how a fine ass lesbian couple climbed their way to the top of the drug world.

By mid-spring we had begun to do what a majority of young black men do best when they come across some money – spend it! We splurged! At the dealerships, it was best that we went together due to the deals that the salesmen and owners would force upon us. In early May Juan and I bought brand new Auroras fully loaded with the works while Ricky had to be the odd ball by buying a new Cadillac which too was loaded and decked out. Two weeks later we were blessed with a godfather deal from this guy who owned a Chevrolet lot in Carmel. He sold us each a 99 Tahoe for almost $17,000 apiece and of course our jewelry and clothing game stepped up a bit. We had it all; at this time of course we weren't exactly twenty one yet so we had fake I.D.'s made and every night spot in the city had us on a "more" courteous level when we arrived. I ended up getting an apartment of my own on the west side in the Islands which were nice and low-key luxury townhouses and apartments because I couldn't do this, that and the other while living at my grandmother's house and plus she would've became suspicious of all my cars parked in her driveway. I could've explained one or two with a job that she thought I still had with her brother but … he personally fired me!

My sex rate shot to the moon but the problem with this was that these females were scandalous, shady and gold diggers – this is who I attracted suddenly but I caught on to them instantly. A few of them were the same ones who turned their noses up at me in the past; I'd try to approach them as a gentlemen but they didn't want that, they wanted to get slapped, spoken bad to and treated like whores so that's what I did to a certain extent minus the smacking or hitting. All I had to do was pull up next to one and let my car call them bitches and hoes and instead of noses getting turned up panties and bra's ended up in my lap – a damn shame! It was funny at first but after a while it got played out because I had to be careful; these girls were twelve pieces and a few had game which forced me to throw up a guard. I had to build a barricade around my heart because I'd be damn if I caught feelings for a hood rat sack chaser or suburban sack chaser for that matter. Who would've known what a necklace, rims and style could do to make females go overboard – I'm talking threesomes, girl on girl and things that I never knew existed. My intentions were not meant to hurt any of these girls but they were molded into what they were – their minds were programmed to target green paper with dead presidents pasted on it just like myself. It was a shame that it took me to get into a car accident just to find a non-gold digger.

CHAPTER 8

May 2000

It was a late afternoon on a gorgeous Thursday when I ran a few errands for my grandmother, the grocery store being one in particular. My sister, Theresa aka Terri decided to tag along with her big brother for the evening. She was sixteen then but of course she didn't look it one bit. The girl had the body of a woman over twenty-five which was the phenomenon of our era thanks to what was being injected into our food.

Some said that she resembled Lisa Raye but I highly disagreed however she did own dark vanilla skin that was as smooth as wax, she stood close to 5'5 and had grown a chest and butt overnight. To make matters worse she composed a fierce attitude that said she was well over the legal age not only that but if she pulled her jet black hair into a ponytail and pronounced a verb with our Mother's French Quarter accent then I would've sworn that my mother and her were the same person. Terri was beyond smart and loved to write, she always spoke about becoming a writer for a big time magazine or newspaper and of course I would always push her forward with her dreams. My brotherly skills had to of paid off because she knew how to handle herself when it came to boys and she knew the definition of the word priority. She was on the right path to becoming an excellent woman, I mean yeah she was at that age where she was exploring dating, sexuality and all that but she was on point for the most part.

We had just finished up with the last of Moma's shopping list and all the checkout lanes were packed so by me being me I stood in the lane where the cutest cashier stood. I glanced at a tabloid that said J-lo was being extorted by Suge Knight over a sex tape and at that moment I could only wish to see that tape.

"Where did you get that shirt girl, I didn't buy that." I nodded to her cleavage baring Ralph Lauren.

"Moma bought it for me."

"Yeah right, tell me anything." I thought that I was speaking in a low whisper but obviously not.

"I think it's cute, I like it." An exotic voice chimed in.

I looked behind me following the voice that saved my sister's life and my eyes flickered from this girls smile. Terri and she were smiling at each other as if they were best friends, and I couldn't speak while looking at her. She owned dark sand brown hair that laid clearly past her shoulders, honey hazel eyes with full lush lips and her skin could've only been produced in South America somewhere. The more that I rudely stared at her the more familiar she looked. Her breast forced the gold D&G logo to expand a bit and her butt did a similar routine with the blue jean logo stitched on her left back pocket, she didn't wear a gram of make-up or maybe lip gloss at the most.

"Well Terri, I think that this pretty lady just offered to take you home."

"Sure. She can ride with us since you're acting as if you don't know anyone." She placed her hand on her hip in attitude.

I was lost and my face said it all while she continued to grin at me. I happened to glance around her leg and noticed her man – he was every bit of three feet with a tanned caramel skin and a face as innocent as could be. His little arm gripped his mother's leg while his other wandered through the candy rack.

"Christopher, please put that down, you have plenty at home."

And that's when it hit me like a Mack truck; his name, her manicured fingers – could never forget those things that nearly cut my circulation off nearly two and a half years ago.

"Zanada? Yeah right!"

She was all smiles when I pulled her in for a hug; her scent simply matched her beauty – fruit and vanilla is what I guessed and her touch was chilling. I pulled back and introduced her to Terri.

"Told you that he was going to be a little heart breaker."

"Yeah, he's my little heart breaker alright." She ran her hand through his thick wavy hair. The baby boy had her eyes, ears, nose and eyebrows all down to an exact match. The only thing that he was lacking was her skin tone which wasn't far off from my own. I'd pay for all of our groceries and chat on the way out. The sun had just about vanished when we strolled out to the parking lot. She was driving a black later model Grand Cherokee with a light tint, my sister pulled up next to us in my Aurora right as I was about to try my luck with the girl. At that moment I only knew that her looks and attitude were both beautiful but I knew nothing else about her but I'd take a chance though.

"So, are you living out this way?"

"Yeap. Down the street in Hunters Run." She pointed south.

"That's cool. You like it?"

"Yeah, it's okay, a little busy but okay. What about you?"

"Kind of. She and my grandmother live down the street off Michigan Rd but I live a little further west on Dandy Trail." I pointed west while leaning on her door. "Is it just the two of you there?"

"Is that your way of asking if I have a man?"

"Maybe." I grinned.

"Umn humn, I bet." She smiled.

"Mommy I hungry."

"Okay baby, we're on the way home." Her focus went from her son back to me, "What about you, do you live with someone?"

"Yeah, my fish." Shaun popped up in my head and that quick I erased her from it, "And we're bachelors."

She shot me her signature smile once again. "A bachelor hunh … well you should call me sometime Mr. Bachelor."

"You know what … I just might be able to do that." I teased her while she retrieved a pen and piece of paper from her purse.

"Here's my home and cell, call me sometime." She blushed as I closed her door.

"Okay, will do." I kept my composure as we said our goodbyes. I sat in the passenger seat of my car trying to figure out why I suddenly felt like I had found my soul mate … my ass was glowing. Terri saw it and simply shook her head as she drove off. I turned the music up allowing the soulful sounds of Carl Thomas' Emotional blasting through my Kenwood's.

CHAPTER 9

The fall came like a bat out of hell.

I had no clue as to where the summer went; I was in the streets super heavy during the summer and made a killing. Money wasn't an issue any more and my cliental had become steady and diverse as ever; I'm talking about people who thought society would never dream of smoked crack – physicians, CEO's, truck drivers, correctional officers and even a state prosecutor who spent close to fifteen hundred every three weeks. They were all human too, no one was perfect and not only that but this was their business. I just provided the need that they lurked for. Their secret was kept a secret dealing with me.

Ricky and I met up with Juan back in 96 during my freshmen year of high school and Ricky was a sophomore. Juan lived clear out on the east side before he moved to our neck of the woods. We met him on the bus stop on a chilly morning during the second semester. He seemed like a real cool brother like ourselves so throughout the school year he became like a brother to us. Ricky and I had history since we were seven; we'd been aces ever since then. If you saw him then that meant that I wasn't too far away, or, vice versa. I had his back and he had mine. However, Ricky ended up going his own way at the end of the summer because he claimed that he couldn't make the type of money that he "should" have been making in our hood, so, he migrated to the south side with his cousin. I didn't want him out there at all because I knew nothing about that side of town but he assured me that he and his cousin could sew things up out there. No hard feelings came about; I had to let him do him. We'd continue to kick it and stunt together but our business changed; we still had the same connect but he handled his own while Juan and I still went in half together.

I told my people and new friend that I scored a job at Pepsi working forty hours a week which in a way was the truth but instead of forty hours I worked maybe fifteen and only three days out the week, my sister knew what was up and Shaun wasn't born in a barn.

I was starting to spend quite a bit of time with my new friend. We were starting to become an item and I wasn't minding it one bit. I was skating on thin ice because Zanada and I were going to places that could've easily ran me up but it was like I didn't give a damn. However, I did find myself talking my way out a few "where have you been's" and "why haven't you been answering your phone's." I worked through those due to my quick thinking and lying skills. Zanada easily passed the hood rat/gold-digger test a week after we united. Something had to be up with me because three months had passed and she hadn't come up off her goods yet. Any other time I would've put the girl in the wind. I never had to wait three months for sex – come to think about it I never waited longer than three weeks except for Shaun and she held me at bay for about a month.

Her spirit was one of a kind and I loved being around her. I remembered my grandmother saying that a man has found something wonderful when a woman is beautiful inside and out and it was a hard package to find so when you find that then … hold on to it.

Zanada would tell me the tragic story about her mother who was born in South America, she had been killed by a drunk driver on the interstate. Zanada was fifteen at the time. She didn't go into big detail about the accident which I understood because we shared similar losses. Her father, a black man who was born and raised here, felt responsible for his wife's death being that he initiated the argument that sent her on the miserable drive to cool off that night. She loved her father whole heartedly and would constantly remind him that it wasn't his fault. He'd then tell his only child thank you for not blaming him but after realizing how much his daughter and late wife resembled he'd begin to drink his pain away. Although the father and daughter team would tough it out together. He was a single father raising a teenage girl which was tough on its own but he did it for the most part. She left home when she found out that she was two months pregnant, she was twenty-one then. She graduated from Ben Davis and for some odd reason she put her college dream on hold. She still maintained steady employment at National City bank where she'd climb the ladder from a teller to an operations manager – the girl had it going on and that turned me on.

CHAPTER 10

Shaun and I were having lunch on a Monday afternoon at a local bar and grill in the heart of downtown when I received her call. Whoever came up with the idea of putting a vibrator on the phone was a saint! I excused myself and darted to the men's room.

"Hello …"

"Hey, what's up?" She sounded excited.

"Nothing. Running a few errands. What's up with you?"

"Do you have any plans for tonight?"

"Not that I know of."

"Good. That means that these tickets for tonight's game won't go to waste then."

"What game –Colts?" I got excited.

"Yeap, my boss gave them to me and he said that the seats are great."

"Don't even trip, we're there. What time – wait … you like football?"

"Are you serious, I use to play football! Kickoff is at 8:15 so be at my place around 7'ish."

"Aight, coo."

After that quick phone call I eased back into our booth by the window that overlooked Illinois street. Shaun smiled at me and said:

"You okay?"

I told her that I was fine without looking her in the eyes.

***

By 7:15 I was knocking on her door ready for some football. I hadn't been to a colt's game in years which is why I had no choice but to go buy a jersey with a matching hat. She answered the door wearing a gold and black scarf around her head, a violet Ben Davis t-shirt and a pair of plaid boxers. Her place stayed immaculate which I took heed to the first time I visited her.

"You look nice. Make yourself at home, I'm almost ready."

"Thanks. I thought that you were wearing that."

"Ha, you're funny." She smiled at my sarcasm. When she made her way to her room I was able to catch a nice view of her body; her legs were so smooth and freshly shaved and they were well-defined similar to a woman who knew a bit about track and field. Her butt simply protruded right through her loose-fitting boxers and all I could do was nod my head while tossing one of her son's toys in the air.

"Nice draws by the way. Did one of your boyfriends leave them?"

"Actually no. I bought them for one of my boyfriends." She hollered from her room.

Damn, nice come back, I thought.

Her door cracked open a bit and she stood partially between it enough for me to see her white bra and tight-fitting blue jeans. She threw a package at me; a three pack of multi-colored Nautica boxers with a pair missing.

"I was thinking about you earlier."

"Thank you. So … I'm your boyfriend now?"

"I guess so." She giggled.

"So … just like that I'm your man – I don't get any say so?"

"Nope, sorry." She laughed again. I did the same.

"Okay, well since we have that taken care of when do you think that I could have my other pair of boxers?"

"I guess when you decide to come and get them."

If we weren't on the way out then I probably would have messed around and taught her a lesson about writing checks that she couldn't cash. Moments later she waltzed out the room in a white feminine shirt that bore a blue Siamese cat on her left upper breast with matching indigo jeans. Her petite feet were well cushioned by a pair of white and blue air-maxes and I had just the thing to top her sexy style off. She'd reach for her jacket and purse and pause:

"Am I driving?"

"Doesn't matter, I'll drive or can I drive your car – I want to see what all the hype is about."

"Sure."

"Hold on real quick then." I ran to my car to grab the small bag, and we left.

***

"Why'd you get rid of the Cherokee again?" I opened up her new Lincoln L.S. going east on the 38th street ramp.

"Don't know. Got tired of it I guess."

"Oh, almost forgot. Here you go." I handed her the small bag, "I was thinking about you earlier." She'd grin and reach over to peck me on my cheek. She put the twin version of my hat on.

"Let me see, I guessed on the size."

"Good guess. It fits perfectly." She looked so damn sexy in it.

***

The Colts won by a field goal; twenty-four to twenty-one. Jacksonville gave them a run for their money but couldn't hold them off in the end. We had a blast that night, the entire RCA Dome wore blue and white and the noise in that place was insane. The drive home was quiet at first due to our sore vocals after all the yelling and cheering we did. I took the scenic route back to her place until I questioned her:

"You hungry?"

"A little bit" she answered in a raspy tone.

I eased my way to a Steak-n-shake drive thru where we spoke about little nothings such as who was famous that banked at her bank; her girlfriend who was nerve wrecking and how fast her son was growing. I watched her speak as the street light luminesced her gorgeous face; her lips, her nose, her hair and how it hung down both sides of her hat. She didn't notice my staring although I noticed something about her. She owned a small beauty mark on her lower left cheek. The girl defined beauty to another level. On the way home she'd help feed me bites of my burger and fries which was cute on her behalf.

"Javon, what about your father, is he in your life?" she asked out of nowhere while we sat at a stop light. "Nawh. He ain't nowhere to be found, don't know who he is." I answered nonchalantly.

"You don't know him or you don't want to know him?"

"Don't know him. Don't know his name, age, social security number – don't know shit 'bout him." I snapped.

"Maybe you can try to find him?"

"How? My mother is dead, my grandmother doesn't have a clue of who he is and my sister obviously has a different father." I snapped again.

"I'm sorry Javon, I'm so sorry."

"For what? Don't be sorry. It's no longer a big deal – fuck him. I've made it this far without him and I know that I'll never do my kids like that."

"Well, whoever he is sure is missing out on a wonderful young man." She glanced into my eyes while reaching for my hand.

I grinned while hesitating on my next question.

"Let me ask you something while we're on the subject?"

"Okay."

"Where's your sons father and why in the hell wasn't he there when you had him?"

She turned her head towards the window.

"Christopher's father is gone, long gone. He's in prison." She paused. "He chose not only the streets over me but another girl as well." She released my hand. "He was a liar, manipulator and he portrayed someone who he wasn't."

"That's messed up, I'm sorry. What did he get sent up for?"

"Drugs and attempted murder."

"Damn. How much time he get?"

"Like fifty years."

"Shit! That's crazy. Does he call, write or do you ever visit him?

"No. I've moved twice and changed my number three times just to keep him and his family out of our lives." Her voice held worry. I wondered why she'd do that to that man. Regardless their issues the boy was his just as much as he was hers. The man made some mistakes but damn. I began to wonder if that was the type of thing that happened with my mother and father.

"Is that why you had Christopher at the mid-wife place instead of the hospital?"

"As bad as it may sound, yes. But try not to look at me in a negative way, you'd never understand exactly."

"I wouldn't do that. You had to do what you had to. I'm just sorry that he did you like that."

"Don't be. His lost not mine." She sarcastically chuckled.

I cracked the window and turned the music up as I let our emotions and anger seep out into the night's atmosphere. Minutes later I pulled up in her designated parking spot and killed the engine.

"Javon, let me ask you a question …"

"Yes ma'am."

"Are you a liar?" Her eyes locked into mine but I was such a good liar that I stared back at her and told her no. "Good because I like you and I dont like a liar." Silence passed us before I walked her to her door. That perfect time came and I'd kiss her goodnight but I think she found herself a little caught up because not only did she lose her breath but she wanted more.

I pulled back from her and said "Well, Lil moma, you better gone on in and get yourself some rest for work tomorrow."

"Actually, I'm off." She said seductively while biting her bottom lip.

"Must be nice."

"You have to work?"

"Something like that."

"You can stay for a little bit, can't you?" She'd pull me in by the hand without my approval.

She messed around and fixed us a night-cap; Grey Goose and pineapple juice. I didn't even know that she drank hard liquor, fooled my ass. We small talked on knick-knack topics again while the Soul Child serenaded us about knowing if the girl next door would have been her. Silence intervened until she giggled. I snickered. Effects from the alcohol I assumed but what happened next was how it all began. She chose to climb on top of me in a semi-straddle; my heart skipped a rhythm.

She kissed me, a light sensual turned into a heated aggressive and that triggered it all. Heavy panting … our shirts came off … her chest pressed against mine … she teased my neck with her tongue and if she knew any better than she would've left my neck alone, but obviously …

"Girl, do you realize what you're doing?" I whispered. No answer from her. She was entirely too caught up in the moment. I went for what I knew like an animal in the wild trying to survive. I returned more kisses around her neck while unfastening her bra with one hand; I eased down to her breast taking my time on each supple one. She'd squirm a bit while I could taste her fruit and berries body wash as I traveled further south to her stomach. I was surprised to see how flat and firm her tummy was. I eased her jeans off one leg at a time and then started to lick up and down her inner thighs; she'd moan as I teased her thin crème thongs off. I tasted her … she tensed … I journeyed my tongue through her world, her inner world. Through her soul, her inner soul. She grabbed my head forcefully and cried in bliss. We'd soon trade positions; I maneuvered back onto the couch where she yanked my jeans off, she'd grab me and begin to jerk more blood into my third leg and soon after she started to return the oral favor. She tossed her hair to one side while softly maneuvering her jaw bone; I felt her hand start to juggle my nuts – I stopped her right as I felt a trickle of a rush coming.

"Come on." She led me to her bedroom.

We were naked and the Soul Child could still be heard. I noticed her clock glowing in red on her night stand. 1:07 a.m.

I had her on her back with my left hand palming her lower back kissing her while testing her waters – her breathing and soft moans picked as she grabbed me. She took control by guiding me into her, it took a moment for her to completely accept me but she'd complete the task. It started slow and easy until her body conformed to me a little better but things then turned into divine ecstasy as our pace sped up … in and out … in and out … deep long thrusts inside her … heavy panting and rapid breathing. Her inner muscles contracted on me and at that moment I knew that I'd become pussy whipped; a shame but true. A condom had somehow bypassed my mind but fuck it! She stopped me and then turned over on all fours with her back in a deep arch as I re-entered her. She became wetter with every thrust and her screaming only fueled the fire of passion.

"Are you okay?" I whispered.

"Yes. Don't stop Javon – no pares."

"I won't."

So many positions in such little time. I laid her on her side crossing her legs to resemble 3:30 and her reaction was this:

"Javon, baby, pegala duro papi – I'm … I'm about to come. Por favor, right there."

No she didn't begin to speak Spanish to me! All that did was make me stroke even harder where she pleaded intensively.

"I'm … coming! Oh god …" She kept me locked inside of her while suddenly reaching her lips to mine, she sucked my bottom so hard that it became numb. She trembled before crashing back down to the queen bed. We were still united as one in the spoon position and our racing hearts spoke a foreign language to one another.

"Did you …" She asked in a submissive tone.

I explained that I only wanted to please her and that it didn't matter if I did or not. My response turned her on even more because the festivities were not quite finished yet, she wanted more and I had plenty to go around. She wanted the pillow propped underneath her, she wanted to stand up and bend over; sideways, this way and that way but she absolutely did it when she sat on top of me in the reverse cowgirl position.

She worked her body of perfection and worked it until she leaned back on me and matched rhythms; hers in a hard deep grind taking every single inch of my fighting temptation. She relaxed the back of her head on my chest while I wrapped my arms around her stomach and left breast; I'd grip her as if I were falling. She knew that I was on the verge of eruption. I couldn't hold off any longer; I was surprised that I held off that long any damn ways. I was showboating on accident. I suddenly gasped while squeezing the life out of her; it was time for 6.8 seconds of a feeling that's indescribable. It happened. I released my soldiers off to war and if one of them would have won then so be it. That's how I felt about this girl. We laid next to one another in amazement and exhaustion.

"Now, what were you saying about coming to get those boxers of mine?" I teased her but she didn't answer. "Okay, you can keep them then." She didn't budge. I called her name then raised my head to study her. She was fast asleep like a playful child who had one helluva day. I put the girl to sleep! Her clock read 4:46 a.m. when I dozed off but when I awoke it said 6:15. I dozed back off.

Chapter 11

The Circle City Classic always came around the first or second week of October and the city would be filled with HBCU football fans. Howard and Grambling State would battle it out this go round.

Juan was stuck at the hospital that weekend due to complications with his first-born at birth. I told him that I was a call away if he needed me but he said that everything was cool. I put a prayer in the wind for him and his baby and called Ricky. Ricky was kicking it with his cousin and fella's from out south so it looked as if I'd be solo this classic event. I'd end up letting one of my youngster's stunt and trail me in one of my toys but that would be about it. It was chilly that Friday, maybe 49 degree's if that but a jacket would do me just fine. I'd end up showcasing the 69' Electra drop which was painted a midnight onyx with several clear coats along with a vulgar mural resting on the trunk; a seductive sista in a two piece straddled the airbrush words: *A woman can't get this wet* and under her legs fell droplets of water causing a splash affect. Of course it was rimmed up with a system that disturbed the peace and a few TV's for show.

Every downtown street and sidewalk was in fact packed with fans and locals showboating their vehicles, clothing and so called wealth. Typical. I ended the night by riding out to an after party out west, I kept it simple.

Saturday morning I ran across a pair of comedy show tickets for that night. Shaun was out-of-town on a church event with her mother which she begged me to attend but I promised her that I'd go to the next one. My next move was to take Zanada out on the town. The show started at 9:45 p.m. which allowed me to make reservations for Ricks Boatyard café prior to it. A simple solid Coogi with matching hard boy black jeans and a pair of crème and gum Havana Joes was my selection in apparel; no gaudy jewelry besides my presidential watch and diamond earrings with several squirts of Allure for men and I was good to go.

***

It was dark when I pulled up to her place but not exactly chilly; Indiana weather was odd as hell. Before exiting my truck I noticed a small bag of chronic laying in the ash tray *Rico's ass* I thought before closing it up. She'd answer the door singing and resembling an angel!

"Hey."

"Hey Toni Braxton." I pulled her towards me for a hug.

"Mmn, you smell great – what is that?"

"Awh nothing, some cheap shit."

"Yeah right, you cheap … please."

"Look at you, you look lovely." I twirled her around lusting over her prestigious figure. She wore a long sleeve sand stone V-neck that was practically sheer but her bra was the same color which made the shirt look less sheer. Her crème slacks fit her like a glove while her sand stiletto boots set her off to a perfect ending. The tiny crochet braids that she possessed hung viciously down her back while her accessories worked their magic as well.

"You're not too bad yourself Coogi man."

"Thanks, I try. So, are we ready, reservation is at –"

"7:30. Yes baby, let's go." She reached for her dark chocolate leather off the coat rack before we left.

I'd help her into the Tahoe as she asked: "This is nice, how long have you had it?"

"For a while now, don't really drive it too much though."

"Geez, your job sure is taking good care of you." She said while eyeballing the ashtray.

"If that's what you want to call it."

"Do you smoke a lot of weed?" She opened the ashtray.

"Every now and then. Why?"

"No reason. Just wondered." She'd shrug her shoulders and smell the bag, "I've never been high before – well I don't know because I may have caught a contact before. My girlfriend, the one I was telling you about, well her friend LeAnn smokes non-stop and one day after riding with them I felt weird."

"You've never literally put a blunt or joint up to lips and inhaled?"

"Nope. Never. Why, are you planning on getting high tonight?"

"I doubt – why? Do you want to get high or something?"

"Oh lord no, just wondered." A feminine giggle escaped from her.

***

The show ended a little before twelve and we were still full of energy. The night was breezy maybe 54 degrees at the most but it was still a gorgeous night.

"What time do we have to pick Christopher up?" I questioned as we sat in traffic.

"I'll get him tomorrow; my daddy says that I don't bring him around enough so I'm going to let them have some quality time together."

"Well then … do you have anything in mind?"

"No, not really."

"Can you walk in those?"

"Of course I can – why?"

"Just wondering."

"You're not planning on putting me out, are you?"

"How did you know?" I laughed.

"Okay and I bet you'll be walking right with me, tuh."

I smiled at her comeback while slipping through some minor traffic to find parking on Washington Street in front of the government center. She pointed to the *no parking* sign wrapped around the meter; I pointed to the void after 10 p.m. underneath it.

"Come on, and here … you'll need this." I handed her jacket to her.

We walked the canal path for at least an hour. We talked, flirted and flirted some more – we simply enjoyed one another's company. The girl brought a side of me out that I never knew existed; LaShaun couldn't even bring this side of me out or at least she hadn't yet. I was getting soft.

I showed her the WW2 memorial centered at the canals over path where my grandfather's name and honors were engraved in a plaque. She would then direct me to a unique sculpture that originated from her mother's country, the art museum had donated it to the Eiteljorg museum which was also connected to the canal. We took a seat on a chilly cement bench and kept one another warm as she told me the story of how her mother and relatives fled Asuncion to the states and how they all ended up working at a bedding factory in Ft. Wayne, IN which is where and how her parents met.

As the night progressed we found ourselves kissing frequently like a teenage couple would do every chance that they could get. A few other couples did the same although I had to wonder what brought them out on a night such as this one possibly the same thing that had us there.

We made our way back to the street which was still a bit crowded. She shivered some while entering the truck; I turned the heat up while pulling off. She'd toy with the c.d. folder before questioning: "What do you know about Sade?"

"No, what do you know about Sade? I was raised on that woman. She hit the volume button and started to chime into the lyrics: *I cherish the day/ won't go astray/won't keep me runnin.*

By 1:56 a.m. Maxwell was crooning to us and yet we were posted back in her parking space. She stared out her window and spoke like a spoiled child: "I'm not ready to go home; I'm having a wonderful time with you."

"Ok. Fine." I hit my lights and pulled back off. Five minutes later we pulled into the Islands.

"The fountain is beautiful, it's beautiful out here period – it's expensive, isn't it?"

"It isn't too bad, I get free cable!"

She'd giggle her signature laugh before exiting the truck, "Wait, one question." She paused.

"What's up?"

"Why am I just now coming to your place?"

"You never wanted to."

"Hmn."

"Come on girly."

She was in shock after witnessing the inside of my place, before I flipped the lights on the moon light beamed straight through the skylight to cast a gorgeous reflection off my four-foot octagon aquarium.

"Here, let me put this up for you."

My place was more than fit for a guy who was a bachelor. A naval blue leather sectional rested against the back wall and across from it stood a 52 inch RCA with surround sound; and to the left by the sliding porch door was the house system that could've probably evicted me if turned on mid volume. I'd give her a brief tour of my bedroom, bathrooms and kitchen which were all laid completely out.

"Okay, so … which one of your little girlfriends helped you with this place?"

"Yeah right, this is all my work – are you saying that a man can't have good taste?" I defended myself while pressing play on my remote.

"No, not at all but … you did an excellent job … wow!"

"Thanks."

"Do you mind if I take these off? My feet are killing me."

"Please make yourself at home. Can I get you something to drink?"

"Sure. I'll have whatever you're having."

"You sure cause I'm goin' in the paint?"

"I'm going in the paint with you then." She smiled.

I grinned and asked her if she was hungry, she wasn't. As I poured our drinks I thought about how much of a gift this girl was, it was unreal almost. She was amazing but … I still had Shaun wrapped around my finger. I had to do something about it but what?

"Here you are ma'am, do you need anything else?"

"No thank you, this is perfect."

I watched her sip from the glass expecting to see her fret from the vodka. She surprised the shit out of me by sipping it like water.

"Goose?" She sipped again.

"You already know."

"This is good –"She burped, "eeww, excuse me."

She forced me to laugh at her silliness.

"Hey, can we smoke this?" She opened her hand showcasing a sack of chronic – the sack from my ash tray! I knew I wasn't hallucinating when I thought I saw her hand reach for it.

"What! Thought you said that you don't get high?"

"I don't. But there's a first time for everything and I feel comfortable doing it with you."

"Are you drunk?"

"Are you serious? Drunk from what, this?" She waved her glass in front of me and finished it off.

I nodded, "Sooo … you want me to roll this up?"

"Yes."

"And you want to smoke it?"

"Yes."

"Okay. But I better warn you first; this isn't the average weed. This is indough, the female plant and she is potent as hell."

"Okay." She handed me the sack.

"Okay." I made my way to the back to find a liquorice paper and ash tray. I sat next to her; lit it and hit it. "Do you know how to inhale – shit I guess so! Don't hit it that hard, you'll –"She began to cough uncontrollably. "Are you okay? You can't hit it that hard, you'll obviously choke."

"I see." Tears started to build up in her eyes as she continued to cough lightly.

Several moments passed as I finished the joint off and I was high as hell so I could only imagine how she felt. She found everything hilarious and her eyes had turned to a vivacious red hue. I had several magazines scattered along my coffee table: Ebony, XXL, Vibe and Black Tail; out of them all she reached for the Black Tail and began to rudely disrespect the women abruptly. She had me in tears after clowning their bad weaves to their uneven fake tits all the way down to their crusty bunion infected feet. The girl was indeed funny as hell. We calmed down after a while but by then we were laid up on the couch; my feet propped up on the glass as her head rested on my lap. Just as soon as I thought that she was dozing off she'd begin to hum to Anita Bakers' Body and Soul that was playing in the back.

"You really that you know good umn … umn …"

"Music?"

"Yes, music. Thank you." We laughed.

"Yeah, I love music."

"Me too." She'd gaze up at the constellations through the skylight, "Are you always this fun to be around?"

"I think the question is are you this fun to be around?"

"The funny thing is that you bring this side of me out. No one really see's this side of me. Javon, I've been hurt before and … I don't – can't go through that pain or emotional rollercoaster again. I mean not to say that you would do that but I'm overly cautious." She glared into my eyes, "We've already done the do in which I expected you to pull a disappearing act afterward but … you didn't. I like you Javon, I like you a little too much I believe. I don't think that we're on the same page though."

"What makes you think that, I haven't given you any reason to think that I'm not feeling you, have I? There's no need to be scared. I think that we're on the same page matter of fact I think that we are on the same paragraph." I grabbed her soft hand, "But remember, you can't categorize me with your past. I'm your present and future, nothing other." I grabbed her tightly and allowed her to inhale my sincerity. I watched her closely until I couldn't hold on any longer, the female plant gave our minds and bodies strict orders to rest. We did.

Chapter 12

It was a Friday still in October when I hooked up with one of my buddies from junior high. Doug Pivine better known as Dougy P was probably one of the realist friends I had. Even though our lifestyles were completely different and we hadn't been close like how we were years ago but that didn't change shit – Dougy was my ace! He was twenty-two with tanned skin and his height and build reminded me of a wide receiver. The boy had women of all shades and colors infatuated with his water chameleon eyes and clean-cut persona. He lived a block north from my grandmothers with his rich ass parents – he was spoiled beyond bad meat! I guess if my father was director of sales at one of the biggest pharmaceutical firms in the Midwest and mom was raking in major dollars from one of those pyramid clubs then I'd be spoiled too!

Doug was in town for that weekend. He attended Notre Dame majoring in finance – like father like son. We would end up hanging out in Broad Ripple that night. Ripple was a small village on the north side that forced hippies, preps, college kids and even some thugs to party throughout the night at its' bars, pubs, restaurants, billiards and clubs scattered through a twelve block radius; north to south, east to west. Forgot to mention that any drug could be found in ripple regardless if it were behind the counter, over the counter, underground or above ground – if you wanted the drug then it was close, if not one person away.

***

A long line awaited us at club Eden. It was nearing 11:30 and the line hosted people of all nationalities awaiting to party. Several blonds gazed at Doug's BMW as we hopped out, I couldn't do anything besides laugh at that fact that a car can get a man pussy, damn shame if you asked me but at least it gets things down to the point. We made it past the bouncer check point and headed straight to the bar. The club had an upstairs, a huge dance floor with three human cages in each corner, three bars and a number of booths along the entire west wing.

"Javon, what are you drinking bro?"

"Goose. No ice."

"Sorry bro but we don't have any –"That was the male bartender.

"Yeah we do, I just brought some bottles from upstairs. You say no ice bro?" This was the female bartender who was a cute tiny brunette with silicon's from here to there.

"Look at all of these freakin' chicks dude! It's like three to every dude." Doug yelled while taking care of the first round.

"You ain't lying." I sipped on my drink.

"Javon?"

"Yo."

"Under your napkin."

I slid my napkin closer to me and slightly lifted it up. A small lime pill with what looked like a fish symbol engraved in it sat all alone. He grinned at me and popped one with a swig of his bud light.

"Is this ..."

He nodded with a grin before ordering another round. I knew nothing about ecstasy besides what a few of the rappers said about it. I heard it was supposed to be a sex drug that enhanced everything, I didn't really need any help in that area but I figured one time wouldn't hurt. "How does it make you feel?" I yelled over the music.

"Ah shit dude, you've never rolled before?"

"Rolled?"

"Yeah, that's what it's called – it's too cool – its un-fucking believable." That was Ms. Silicone again interfering in our damn business. Her skin-tight black club Eden shirt forced her tits to apologize for being nosey. I asked her name, it was Titty – I mean Tina.

"It's un-fucking believable hunh?" I glanced at it one more time before popping it. I had no fucking clue as to what I had just done, had no clue as what to expect – fuck it, it was done! Twenty minutes later I found myself in one of the booths nursing another round of alcohol with no new or weird feelings yet. Maybe I wouldn't feel shit, maybe the pill was bullshit – who knew! Techno music had the club in a frenzy including myself unless mine was anxiety. I'd notice Doug on the dance floor with a small group of mixed races and sexes. The group quickly disbursed with smirks of copped fixes. I wondered if Doug was involved in more than just a financing degree at school; he saw me looking his way and nodded with a devilish grin. I laughed. Titty – I mean Tina's little frame sat two bottles of Evian in front of me and said: "You'll need these, trust me."

"Thanks baby girl."

"You're most certainly welcome cutie; if you need anything else just let me know okay." Her okay sounded as if it came straight out of the 90210 area code.

My watch read 12:10 a.m. when Doug introduced me to this real cute girl who went to school with him, her name was Erica and she favored that new singing chic with braids who stayed on a piano no matter what. She wore a metallic black dress that simply had sex with her body. Her breasts were amazing and I saw no signs of a pooch. I couldn't see her back side yet but I imagined that it had to be something back there. After our introduction she surprised me by sitting across from me.

"Can I get you a drink, Erica?"

"Yes please, a Shirley Temple please." Her voice was professional, crisp and yet sweet.

I flagged Tina down and quickly remembered what a Shirley Temple consisted of, "You don't drink?"

"Yes, I do but I'm driving tonight." She grinned with confidence.

"That's cool, you're responsible. Tina, a Shirley Temple for the pretty lady and another MGD please."

"Coming right up." She pranced off.

My focus shot back to Erica and suddenly I noticed something about her – her eyes were a sea green that spoke miracles; if they were hers then this girl was truly blessed – if they weren't hers she was still truly blessed! "So do you come here often?"

"Actually this is my second time here. It's okay here but I prefer the Vogue."

"Yeah, I like the Vogue too. Let me ask you – "Her giggle cut me short, "What?"

"I love your accent, where are you from?"

"Accent? I don't have an accent, I'm from here."

"Oh. I'm sorry. Your words sound a little country. It's not a bad thing though, sorry if I offended you."

"I'm not offended, surprised but not offended." I spoke as our drinks were dropped off. "By the way, has anyone ever told you that you resemble –"

"Alicia Keys?"

"Guess so." We celebrated with a light laugh. "Who did you come here with?"

She pointed to several sexy females on the dance floor getting it in.

"You dance?"

"Of course."

I attempted to reply when all of sudden something crazy started to happen to my body. It became relaxed and limber, it felt wonderful and my hearing took on a new sound of clarity; I could hear every single chime, percussion and word to J-Lo's *Waiting for Tonight*. This was obviously the x pill doing its thing but the scary thing was that it intensified by the minute.

"Are you alright?"

I gazed at her attempting to regain my composure but couldn't. This was crazy. The strobe lights, bar signs and glow sticks twirling all played illusions on my eyes.

"Javon, are you okay?"

"Hunh … yeah, I'm fine."

"What's wrong, you seem …"

"Nothing is wrong besides the fact of how gorgeous you are."

Her blush was camouflaged by her smile that could easily refresh any stormy day. The pretty little thing had my full attention, nothing else in that club mattered at that moment. For that next ten minutes my high was shooting straight to the moon and so was our conversation although until this day I can't quite recall what all we discussed but whatever it was she had to of enjoyed it. I remember dancing with her and I don't think that I had ever danced like that before in my life; it was like the music was doing something inside my body. Oh and I remember her having a great ass from grinding behind her. Things became weird though; I quickly became anti-sociable out of nowhere as my jaws became tight and I couldn't stop gritting my teeth. I had to oddly excuse myself from the girl to get Doug's attention.

"What's up bro?"

"Man … I'm … fucked up."

"I see! Your eyes are damn near purple!"

"You ready to bounce?"

"You ready to leave?" He asked in disbelief.

I had to get out of that environment immediately and I think he knew what I meant because moments later we were heading out.

***

I could remember the traffic on Broad Ripple Ave being at a standstill. The party goers were coming and going and they were live! I remembered glancing at his clock and how the numbers 150 teased my vision with green tracers. I looked away from his clock and instantly it hit me, a rush of sexual euphoria cruised through my soul. I couldn't recall being that horny in my life; it was crazy! My mind self-sufficiently went into booty call mode. I could've easily called a hood rat, could've easily went home to wake Shaun up but what if she had a "headache" or some shit – she loved that line "Javon stop, I'm tired and I have a headache." So I would go ahead and try my luck with Zanada without thinking anything about it.

"Hello." Her voice sounded partially sleep.

"Damn, did I awake you?" I whispered.

"Nope, laying down watching TV. What are you doing at this hour?"

"Leaving the Eden in Ripple. My buddy came home for the weekend so we decided to do the club scene."

"Why are you whispering?"

"Hunh, oh sorry. But yeah, I was just checking on you."

"Mmn hmn, its almost two o'clock in the morning and you're checking on me? This sounds more like a booty call to me playa."

"No, no booty call. I respect and love you too much for that."

"I'm sorry but what did you say?"

"Nothing. Well, I'm going to let you get back to your show." I was talking entirely way too much.

"Javon, I'll see you in a few minutes?"

"Yes."

***

An intensifying ten minute ride had me in a state of utopia. Each deep bass beat from Doug's system left me feeling as if I were literally inside the speakers. "Does this shit come down? I'm messed up still."

"It'll mellow out in a bit but you will probably feel it in the morning too. Keep drinking water though."

"Damn! Why didn't I get that girls number! I left her with no bye or nothing'"

"Dude, I got you. You forgot I go to school with her."

"I did. Yeah, let me know what's up with her."

"Got you bro."

"This is it right here bro. All right man, I'm out. We got to do this again – when you going back to South Bend?"

"Sunday afternoon."

"Alight bro." We shook before I exited his foreign toy.

I knocked lightly before she quickly opened the door shielding herself behind it. She greeted me with open arms as usual and no sooner than I viewed her my hormones went deeper into over drive. Her hair; wrapped in a Spanish gold scarf that explained her exotic facial definition; her breast were supported by a crimson lace bra that proved 36 c's weren't too big nor too small. I couldn't help but to palm her soft and perfect ass thanks to her matching boy shorts. Her scent, that feminine berry traveled through my nasal glands to trigger my lips towards hers. She smiled, glanced into my soul and said: "How was the club?"

"It was okay. Typical club scene I guess."

"You hungry?"

Food was the last thing I could think of, however, thirst was another issue. "No thank you but may I have something to drink please?"

"Of course."

I followed her sway to the kitchen: "Sorry to call you so late, I –"

"You should be because I am no one's booty call."

"I know, you're right, no one's booty call besides mine." I teased as she shot me an evil grin. "Is it hot in here or is it me?" I unbuttoned my shirt before downing my water.

"You're hot? I thought that it was a little nippy in here."

I'd ignore her while glancing into her son's room through his cracked door. He was a handsome little fellow and yet the baby boy had no father in his life. At his age he probably didn't understand but I easily did. I'd been there – I knew what it was like to have no father. I felt for him ahead of time, unless, depending on where our relationship would go. Her TV gave off enough light to give her room an indigo tint but I begged her to turn a soft lamp on because my eyes were playing serious games on me. We would discuss the issue about her son which amazed her slightly.

"You wouldn't mind helping me raise my son?" Her attention left the TV right to my eyes.

"Of course not, I'd enjoy that and if I'm with you then he is mine anyways."

"So does this mean that you're planning on being around for a while?"

I smiled as her dimples popped in, "You really like me hunh?"

"I didn't say all that now." I grinned again. "Damn, it's hot in here." I pulled my shirt off.

"Are you high?"

"No, why?"

"Because your eyes look weird."

"Had a few drinks at the club – damn let my eyes have some business of their own." I raised up to stretch after she attempted to kick me.

I noticed the king of R&B's Tp2.com cd laying in front of her cd player, I'd put it in and let it ride out.

"You never told me what happened that night." She pointed to the scar below my right collar-bone.

"I didn't?"

"No."

I was by then sitting in-between her legs gripping her soft hands. "I'll tell you about it later."

"Does it bring back bad memories or something?"

"No, it's just a long ass story."

She would drop it with ease, I loved that about her. She never pushed an issue unless it was absolutely necessary.

"Can I crack the window?"

"Sure. Are you feeling okay? I don't think that it's hot in here."

"I'm fine, I'm just … "I inhaled the fresh air from the night's breeze and mentally left the planet for a good minute. I was so far gone into the night and music that a bomb could've exploded and I wouldn't been fazed at all. I was gone to a place where only feel good medicine existed but I was taken away from it as soon as a pillow was chucked at me.

"Javon, what is your problem?"

"Hunh, what? Sorry, I was thinking about something – what did you say?"

"Never mind now."

"All … you mad? Come here baby."

"What?"

"Come. Here." I held my hand towards her.

She eased herself off the bed and I watched her every move as her ab's slightly winked at me. The girl was fucking amazing; her legs, hips, skin – she was past gorgeous. For some odd reason she resembled Chili that night only off by a slight hue. I was turning into a sucker when it came to her.

She took my hand as I pulled her into me. "Since I've met you my life has changed for the better. Didn't think that I could care for a girl like I do about you. I'm feeling the hell out of you; love your personality which is one of a kind, you're independent, you're an excellent mother and you listen to me. There's no point in lying, I'm kind of new to this boyfriend/girlfriend thing and my past ain't squeaky clean but for you I'm willing to try my best." The x pill had me on a fucking roll.

"For some reason I trust you and I don't trust many people. When I bumped back into you at the grocery that evening I knew that it was for a reason, God allowed us to cross paths again and I knew right then that I wasn't going to let you get past me. You're different and I love how you're full of life. You are gentle, loving, exciting and you're funny as hell but most of all your heart is humongous." She'd stroke my face with her fingertips. The girls words had touched me, she made me feel like a man; a man who needed to be reminded every now and then that he is more than a sperm donor, a financial resource, punching bag and whatever else we're labeled as. The king of R&B kept the mode perfect with the joy he felt and that song alone put me over the edge especially as I noticed her nipples piercing through her bra.

"Did you say that you loved me earlier?"

"Hell no, I didn't say that but if I did, what?" I grinned.

"That's what I thought you said, well guess what?"

"What?"

"I love you too."

We took off into each other's eyes. My body was lusting for hers as hormones overruled and somehow someway kissing always led to bigger and better things. At first I had her propped up on her oak dresser straddling her legs smothering her exterior with kiss after kiss. Her breathing sped up as I quickly unclasped her bra; I teased every curve and nerve of her breast with a simple flick of my tongue. I pulled my head up to her neck to test my vampire skills and she'd automatically slide her hand down my pants. Our chest pressed up against one another, more tonsil soccer as I eased her infamous boy shorts off; I teased her insides with one then two fingers – she was soaking wet. She was past ready. She'd moan and grip my dick harder with speed. I squatted down to instruct her legs to wrap around my neck; my mouth was even with her sex. I placed my arms underneath her thighs and ass while my hands gripped her lower back, I raised her 135 pound frame with ease and her distinctive shriek and giggle said that she was more than thrilled. Her thighs clinched around my cheek bones as my tongue moved throughout the folds of her labia. I continued to follow her bodies orders while she whimpered and left earth, my tongue navigated its way to her south side of the flooded city, it enjoyed every single drop and taste of her rain. My tongue had a mind of its own that night and it was out to educate.

"Oh god … boy what are you doing to me – I'm about to …" The squeeze and grip said it all but her orgasmic hymn signed the deal. I laid her on the bed, cut the light and TV off and the last thing that I remembered was the king of R&B telling us things about the greatest you, the greatest me, we had found the greatest chemistry.

That next morning I awoke to the aroma of breakfast which was always a tale sign. I felt fine but I had to regroup and think about where the hell I was; whose bed was it and why was I naked but all of that was until I heard her ask him to turn the TV down a bit. I found my boxers and shirt and peeked through the door to see Christopher fully dressed sitting Indian style watching Saturday morning cartoons. I crept to the bathroom to take a leak and at least gargle some toothpaste but to my surprise laid a toothbrush and wash cloth set on the sink. She was changing the sheets when I walked back in. Her dimples popped in: "Good morning Mr. Freak. I made breakfast."

I helped her with tucking the sheets, "Mr. Freak?"

"Yes."

"What happened, what did I do?"

"I think the question is what didn't you do?"

I grinned while studying her briefly deciding that she could go to sleep one way and wake up looking the same, only a few could do that. She bent down to grab a pillow which left me no choice but to gaze at her ass that had the word *juicy* printed on her shorts.

"Juicy hunh, they ain't lying."

She smiled. "Can I have a kiss please?"

"Nope."

She stretched across the bed to kiss me, "Do you have plans today?"

"Uh … not until tonight. Tonight is fella's night."

"Really, what all does that consist of?"

"Why, what's up?"

"Well someone keeps nagging me about seeing a zebra and I wouldn't mind seeing a lioness."

"I get the picture. Isn't it cold outside, too cold for the zoo?"

"It's 60 degrees right now."

"It's 60 and almost November. Wow. Okay, the zoo it is."

CHAPTER 13

By 6:30 the sun setting resembled a piece by Norman Miller on canvas. Our day had been filled with live and stuffed animals, race cars and other boyish knick-knacks while our stomachs had been filled with pizza and bread sticks.

I glanced at her as she opened up her Lincoln south bound on Allisonville road; her eyes hollared happiness and at that moment I believed that it had been a while since she felt that. I surfed through her radio to catch the local DJ's announcing every party and shindig jumping off that night. Ten till seven came around when we crossed over 38th and Lafayette road and the sun had vanished but the earth allowed a glow across the western skyline. The baby boy was stretched out across the back seat probably dreaming of zebra's playing skee ball with chuck-e-cheese. Eight blocks later I instructed her to make a right turn where the semi-quiet street viewed the ending of the Eagle Creek small airport which is where we'd watch the last of the days ending flights.

"Pull over right here, the grass won't hurt anything."

This is where I'd tell her that I had been caught up in a drive by shooting not too long ago which made her uneasy for the moment but I had to tell her something. She relaxed when I told her that I had simply been at the wrong place at the wrong time and thought about how that lie would probably somehow come back and kick me in my ass.

"Have you ever thought about moving?" I reclined my seat a bit.

"Like out of town or another side of town?" She reclined as well.

"Out of town."

"Of course, I'd love to move to Atlanta or the east coast; somewhere where there's equal opportunity for us – minorities."

"I agree. This city ain't gonna cut it. You practically have to know someone who knows someone in order to get a decent paying job."

"Yeap."

"So what's stopping you?"

"Let's see … my job, my finances, my father – I can't just leave him, not any time soon anyways. You?"

"I'm ready, ready to go! Atl sounds good and all but … I don't know I'm like you when it comes to my grandmother and sister, can't leave them right now either. Plus my money ain't right. Some people can just up and leave as compared to people who have to plan ahead. I'm an opportunist but I still have to plan ahead. Until this day my grandmother tells me that preparation is one of the keys to life."

"She's right."

"Yeah. I'll see what's up when I get my act together."

"That sounds like a good plan."

We sat in silence briefly watching nothing but the runway lights until a Trojan commercial popped on and I knew what was yet to come.

"Umnn … how come we never use protection?" She questioned calmly.

Those bitch ass commercials do it every single time – they could ruin a wet dream! I had no explanation for her, it was rare that I didn't use them but with her I said what the hell.

"Uh … I don't like how they feel."

"Hunh? You don't like how they – do you like how it feels to raise a baby or do you like how it feels to sit in the clinic waiting on a penicillin shot?"

"Whoa, whoa slow down, hold up … you asked me the question and for one I don't fuck around with a lot of chicks and if I did then I'd use protection. Second, your question was how come "we" don't use protection, shouldn't I be asking you the same question? How do I know that you're not out here doing your thing?"

"But I'm –"

"Hold on, I'm not finished. It takes two to make a baby and if I make one then I will take care of all of my responsibilities unlike a lot of these so-called men. And third, I may had be meddling but weren't those the infamous birth control pills on your dresser?"

Her eyebrow arched, "Can I speak now?"

"Yes, you may."

"Thank you. Yes, those are my birth control pills but they aren't 100% percent effective especially when I forget to take them at times and how do you even know if I'm taking them at all?"

"Then why –"

"Hold on, I'm not finished. Secondly, when I'm involved with someone then I'm only involved with that person. I'm not like these sluts out here, I have morals and I wasn't raised to sleep around with the entire city. I am a lady."

A Rally's commercial played as I took her words in. "Are you mad?" I grinned. She didn't answer. "Zanada, I know that you're a good girl, I knew that when I first saw you. I'm only giving you a hard time because I admire your defense. Wait … was this our first fight?" I brought a smile out of her. "You're sexier when you're upset."

"Shut up boy, I am not upset and don't try to butter me up now."

"Ah you'll get over it – meet me half way." I leaned in towards her.

"Nope."

"No – did you tell me no?" I reached in closer to her forcing a kiss. She couldn't resist. "Well, it's getting to be about that time girl. I told my nigga that I'd be at his spot around ten." Her clock read 8:20.

"Oh. Right, I forget its fella's night." She turned her lights on before fixing her seat. "So what does it exactly consist of?"

Nothing really besides drinking, smoking, strip club – fella's type shit."

"Strip club? You're going to the titty bar?"

"Well, since you put it that way then yeah, the titty bar."

"Hmn." She pouted as we sat at a red light.

"What?"

"Nothing. I could walk … and …" She mumbled while glancing out her window.

"Stop mumbling and say what you have to say."

"I said that I want to go."

"To the strip club?"

"I'm curious to know what the hype is all about. Can I go?"

"Wait, slow down, nothing goes on in there besides topless chick's shaking their asses to loud perverted music, drinking and mingling – you wouldn't enjoy yourself." I tried my best to change her mind but suddenly a light bulb lit up inside my head. Yeah, it would defeat the purpose of fella's night but it wouldn't hurt anything if she went. We were entering my complex when I asked, "So you're dead serious?"

"Yes, I'm serious."

"You wouldn't have a problem watching some chic give me a lap dance?"

"Please … for what?"

"Alight now, don't go changing your mind when some chick has her titty's and coochie all in my face. And what happened to all of your morals and what about church in the morning?"

"Javon, what does morals have to do with going to a strip club, I don't work there and I don't like females in that way. I'm doing it for you and I'll still make it to church in the morning."

"Alright then. But what about him?" I pointed towards the backseat.

"I'm getting ready to drop him off at daddy's then I'm going home to get dressed so you'll be by to get me around what … ten?"

I couldn't do anything besides commend her for her abruptness. "Yeah, ten is good."

***

I called Juan from my house phone as soon as I stepped foot inside. I misplaced my phone somewhere between that day and Doug's car. Didn't know if that was a good thing or not because if Shaun had been calling me, which I knew she had, then that would be a decent excuse for me. Now if I misplaced it within Zanada's reach then would she answer it? I doubted it but when it comes to a woman you never know. I told Juan about the change of plans and he had no complaints because he would bring his little friend Lisa who was down for anything. I told him about the night before with the ecstasy and he acted as if I was late on the memo, I guess he had been rolling for quite some time which I never knew. It just so happened that Lisa's brother was the X man and Juan would grab a few for the night. I'd be clean in a white and blue Enyce long sleeve, jeans and custom blue and white Jordan's. I snatched my chain and Royals fitted cap, a splash of contradiction and I was out the door.

***

"Was my phone in there anywhere?" I questioned her as she stepped up into the truck. She pulled it out of her purse and politely handed it to me.

"Thank you, where was it?" I pulled off.

"On my dresser."

"Your dresser? Damn ... I must have ... damn." I couldn't even imagine how I left it there out of all places. "My buddy is coming with us and I think he's bringing his little friend too, so you won't be alone."

"Okay."

It was eleven on the dot when we pulled up in front of the stash house behind the fairgrounds. Juan usually laid his head here being that no dope was ever sold here, it was a money house. Lisa's heels clacked as she strutted her 5'8 150 pound frame in a pair of skin-tight jeans. Her jacket hid her breast bearing shirt for the moment but any blind man could see her neck length fire engine red hair from a mile away and her dark mahogany skin and almond eyes allowed her to resemble a china doll of color. Did I mention that the girl was a boss freak in the bedroom – Juan never knew about our rendezvous some years back but I didn't think that it was much of an issue being that it was before their time and they weren't in love or anything like that. They were friends with benefits, I guess. Juan's R. Kelly looking ass trailed her grinning from ear to ear dressed in an all-black Girbaud fit with black Timbs. I almost didn't recognize him, I had forgotten that he cut his hair off.

"Hey Lisa. What's up bro?" I reached back to give him some dap. He'd grip my hand and enclose two tiny objects into it. I already knew what they were. "Zanada, this is Lisa and that's Juan." They exchanged greetings as I switched the DVD off to Cash Money's *Get Ya Roll On*. Juan caught on quickly to my choice in my music and began to roll his fists into a circular motion as Lisa did the same.

Pure Passion was clear across the east side of town, the hole in the wall building housed a healthy crowd that night which wasn't unusual. A few women who weren't dancers nor employees were lingering near dope boys, average Joe's and plenty of perverts. We were regulars there, we knew the entire establishment by name. All eyes were on us as we strolled in. I imagined that some of the fellas were thinking *why bring sand to the beach* or *that's some playa ass shit!* I watched her every move at first just to see her demeanor but she kept her composure while admiring the stage where topless women in strings that barely covered their vaginas gyrated, freaked and popped their bodies to the sounds of *Do it baby stick it baby*. Lisa and Zanada had quite a few observers as well, they could look all they wanted but of course no touching was I how I saw things. Zanada's fine ass wore a baby blue long sleeve v-neck that showed a bit much of cleavage and her black pencil drawn-on jeans didn't do her lower body any justice – I loved everything about this girl.

"Are you drinking?"

"I'm having what –"

"I'm having – yeah I know." We grinned at each other.

Juan and I made our way to the bar while nodding to some of the fellas. "Hey Ms. Thelma, how are you?"

"Good baby, how are ya'll? I see you brought some pretty girls with you."

"Yes ma'am, we did." I smiled. Ms. Thelma had worked at the club since it opened, she was a slender darker lady who was at least forty but the cigarettes bumped her appearance up a good ten years. She ran the bar and oversaw the dancers. I'd make the big order and make Juan pay for it or at least for the first round. The waitress could have easily waited on us but I had to get away for a minute to pop my pill. I had forgotten that Juan gave me two pills, I questioned him on the second pill and he said that it was a Viagra. I laughed at him and gave it back to him, I didn't need that shit. We made our way back and I'd hand her drink.

"Thank you. We were just talking about Passion's thongs – they're cute." She pointed to the stage where a caramel toned dancer who was past voluptuous.

"What? You can't even see the girl's thongs – her ass has taken them hostage." We all laughed at my ignorance. I scooted closer to her and asked her if she was getting a feel for the place.

"Yeah, I can see why you like coming here; food, music, alcohol and plenty of T and A!"

"Pssh … I got that at home with you." I laughed at her. She did the same with a grin.

Thirty minutes later I was anxious as hell waiting on my drug to kick in. Juan and Lisa were off the hook with theirs; they sat in front of the stage tipping like crazy, dancing and kissing – they were feeling their drug! Zanada said that they were having a wonderful time and that the liquor must've had them feeling like that. Only if she really knew the truth. The DJ paused our conversation by introducing a new comer to the stage, her name was Rayne and suddenly a three-piece bass line vibrated the entire club as SWV's Rain came on. Rayne sashayed her petite frame on stage and within a split second I cursed myself for calling her out of her name – petite. The girl was cut with another nationality, her 39-29-40 frame shook explicitly. It was odd because Zanada and I both stopped talking to view this girl.

"She's pretty and her hair is long."

"Yeah."

"She doesn't have anything on you though."

"Well thank you – that may have scored you a few extra brownie points." She grinned.

I smiled back at her noticing the thin golden necklace resting in between her breast. My focus went back to Rayne as by now her being clearly at the top of the pole sliding down upside down with one arm.

"Can you do that?"

"I was just wondering that myself. I might."

I was turned on by that comment. Juan and Lisa were tossing singles at the girl which quickly gave me an idea. "Do you want to go over there and tip her?"

"Sure. Let's go."

"Seriously?"

"Yeah, come on."

I finished my drink while handing her half of my singles. We sat two chairs east of Juan and Lisa and no sooner than we sat down Rayne was making her way in front of us. She wore a little too much make up, her tits sat a little too perky and she owned several stretch marks around the inside of her thighs but she was still a ten. She'd give the both of us an exotic gaze and suddenly she was in front of us opening her legs to the point where we could see her vaginal muscles contract through her platinum thong. I felt Zanada's eyes widening as the dancer carried on and no sooner than that occurred I felt that tremendous familiar relaxation travel throughout my body – deja vu. I slouched back in my chair suddenly not having one single care in the world. I stretched, felt like – it was unexplainable. I watched calmly as she placed dollar bills in front of the dancer. Other men seemed to be amazed, probably imagining their fantasies.

"You are so pretty."

"Thank you honey. So are you." Rayne responded to Zanada then turned her body around to where we could witness her backside vibrate rapidly. She'd turn back around cupping and licking her breast. That caused a serious blood rush to my second head.

"Are those yours?"

"Of course they are. I paid for them." They shared a girly smile. Her second song was just about finished which meant her time on stage was near ending. I tucked a handful of ones underneath the edge of her thong while Zanada did the same. She thanked us and went on her way. The horny toads were in their own world still engaging in a session of lip lock, Zanada sent them a look that screamed "get a room" before we sat back down.

"You having a good time Ms. Curious?"

"This is different but I'm with you so I'm having a wonderful time." She knew what to say and when to say it. "May I have another drink please?"

"Of course." I'd flag a waitress down.

We talked about some of the dancer's body styles and what it probably took to open up a strip club, I teased her by telling her that if we opened up one then she'd have to dance first. She laughed in ignorance. Sugar and spice dueled up on stage; Sugar (Leah) was a tanned white girl who had small breast but owned a bottom physique that was unbelievable. Spice (Shatina) was a chocolate tone with a strong hint of Indian, she wore her hair extra low and her body resembled a typical video girls. I had fucked both of them … at the same time. I probably should've never taken her to a damn strip club but she wanted to go, the decision was hers, either she enjoyed it or she didn't which reminded me of when I was a young child and I wanted to taste my granddaddy's beer, he allowed me to taste it alright but he knew that the decision was mine; either I'd liked it or not. I hated the taste. *Vivrant Thang* was playing as I noticed Rayne swaying her hips our way. The drug had suddenly put a picture in my mind of me hitting her from the side with one leg raised in the air. I whispered in Zanada's ear about handling a lap dance and at first she hesitated with an uncomfortable facial but somehow she still agreed to one.

"Hey guys. I came to say thank you for your generous tips."

"You're very welcome sweetie." They smiled at each other. "Umn, may I have a lap dance please?"

"Of course."

I sipped on my water looking onward thinking about how Shaun would've never done that or the entire night. Speaking of the devil, my vibrator went off. The screen read HOME.

One twenty rolled around and I was rolling pretty damn tough, tougher than the previous night. The double stack fish were strong as hell; they had more kick and more energy to them. I started to become agitated from the scent of smoke, varieties of lotions and body sprays and the loudness of booty music. I think we were all ready to go anyways but the new question was could I drive? We loaded up and prepped to bounce, I was good; tough but good.

"Here baby, you control the music." I handed her the remote before pulling off. Lights, seatbelt, window cracked – I was good. I dodged a few sheriffs while cruising back west on 38th street but once I was passed Franklin Road I was even better. "You hungry?"

"I could eat."

"Ya'll hungry back there?" No answer.

We looked in the backseat to see the two lip locked and clothe burning one another. We nodded our heads simultaneously.

"Damn. What is up with them - what did they have to drink?"

"I. Don't. Know. A few too many *sex on the back seats* I guess." Obviously I knew exactly what the issue was.

"I guess so. We better get them home before they get your backseat pregnant." She'd giggle.

We dropped them off and laughed at them as they rushed into the house.

"I hope they make it inside before - well never mind."

"They'll make it, it's too cold out there."

She shot me a look as if I had told the world's biggest lie.

"What?"

"Nothing."

"It is too cold."

"It's never too cold."

"You're a true freak." I grinned.

"Only with you." She licked her lips.

***

I was biting down on the cap to my bottled water to control the gritting of my teeth. She was munching on a piece of pepperoni pizza. We were in a 24 hour pizza shop in Ripple which wasn't too far from the Eden.

"I can't believe that you're not hungry."

"Don't have much of an appetite." Only if she knew why. I went on to lick my lips while admiring her charm.

"What?" She caught me lusting over her.

"What?"

"Why are you looking at me like that?"

"Like how?"

"Like how hell. I know what you're thinking and let me tell you … I did all of this for you tonight. Don't get any ideas of a threesome or something. I'll dance, strip and suck my tits for you but I will not allow another female to intervene with what's mine -"

"But -"

"I'm not finished. We women are beautiful and soft creatures but not enough for me to bump coochies with."

"Calm down baby, I was simply going to compliment your lips but never mind now - you done went clean the hell off on me."

"Oh."

"Yeah, oh." I smiled. "But I'm glad that you let me know about your sexuality. You had me nervous for a minute especially after that lap dance."

"Please. Like I said, I did this for you baby. I'd never mess with a woman."

"Never say never."

"Never." Her shriek made me laugh.

We left that night resembling one of those couples that people would say *awh* to. We walked into my place around a quarter till three and began to pick up where we had left off the night before.

CHAPTER 14

"What's up cutie?"

"Hey baby, how are you?" Her sweet voice replied.

"Good baby, how are you?"

"Great!"

"Well I just called to see what you were doing tonight?"

"Probably go home and cook dinner for my baby and I, why what are you doing?"

"I was going to cook dinner for you two and if you'd like you can take some notes."

"Take notes – from you? Do you even know how to cook?"

"What! Do I know … girl I'm the truth." I finished pumping the gas.

"Okay Mr. Chef Truth, dinner it is. At your place, right?"

"Yep. My place. I have to stop past the store and then I'll be home."

"Okay. See you around sevenish then?"

"Cool."

***

She knocked at the door a little before seven with a white box in her hand.

"Hey. Where's Christ -"

"Boo!" The baby boy popped out of nowhere smiling from ear to ear.

"You scared me man - I like your coat man, can I wear it?"

He'd take it off and hand it to me: "Otay."

"Thanks Chris." I took both of their coats while winking at her. "What's in the box?"

"Dessert." She handed me the box which was easily known as Longs doughnuts.

"Thank you. Sit down. You're at home here." I handed her the remote to the tv.

"Mommy look at the fishee's."

"Yes baby, aren't they pretty."

"Chris do you want to help me feed them later on?"

"Yes please." He answered quickly while glancing towards his mother for approval.

"Javon, whatever that is smells wonderful."

"Yeah, un huh - thank you. Told you that I can cook. Hope you eat pork because I made smothered pork chops with baked potatoes, broccoli and fried corn."

"Sounds amazing."

I'd call for Christopher to come in the kitchen and a second later his little boots came across the kitchen floor. I handed him a toys-r-us bag and told him that the toys were his to keep.

I'd play with him on the floor until dinner wrapped up while she was deep into a show on Lifetime.

An hour had passed since we finished dinner and she couldn't get over the fact that I had skills in the kitchen.

"Baby, I am so sorry for ever doubting your skills in culinary arts." She finished drying a glass off.

"It's okay just focus on cooking for me next time." I handed her a wet plate.

"I don't know, cooking like yours, you might have to cook for me every night."

"Okay, that's coo but under one condition."

"And that is?" She glared at me with her hand on her hip.

"You have to go to the reggae club with me tomorrow night."

"Reggae? You know something about reggae?"

"A little bit. Not a lot but enough. I also have a babysitter for Chris - if that's alright with you?"

"Who?" She backed away from me in defense.

"Terri. My sister, you're buddy, remember?"

"Alright. Reggae club it is."

***

"Goodnight Javon, thank you for everything tonight."

"Anytime baby girl."

"Give me a kiss so I can sleep better."

I stuck my head in her window and just about sucked all the gloss off of her lips. It was close to eleven when she and her son left.

When she pulled off I darted back in the inside to grab my keys and coat. I had to go to my second home and as I pulled up there it looked as if Shaun had just pulled up.

"Hi." She kissed me.

I thought about traces of Zanada's lip gloss after the fact.

"Where have you been?"

"At the car wash. Shooting dice."

She nodded in disgust: "Well did you win us any money?"

"You support my bad habits now?"

"No. Of course not."

"That's what I thought."

"Whatever boy. Are you hungry?"

"No, I'm good. Had some wings from that soul food place next to the car wash."

"Well I am." She put her bag down on the couch and moved to the kitchen.

"Where you been?" I asked defensively.

"School. Duh. Today is Thursday.

"But it's almost eleven-thirty."

"I stopped past my parent's place for a while."

"Oh."

"Are you okay?"

"Yeah, I'm fine. Sorry, I'm tripping." I gave her a healthy hug.

"Whoa Javon … you haven't hugged me like that since … since a long time ago."

I hushed her up by kissing her viciously and grabbing a hand full of her ass. That triggered it. A spark ignited in her eyes, she knew what time it was. I had to give her body and soul the sexual affection that was past due.

CHAPTER 15

That next morning I was up and at it early. I made three quick stops in the 'hood and that quick I counted out three thousand even.

I was at a red light when I thought I saw Juan ride past me. Hadn't heard from him in several days. Figured that I'd call him.

"Yo, what's up bro?"

"Javon the don, what's up with you?"

"Paper chasing."

"Of course. That makes two of us."

"Where you at?" I pulled off.

"Behind you."

I looked in my rearview and sure enough he was behind me.

"Kountry Kitchen?"

"Yep."

"Bet."

***

"How's your son doing?"

"He's doing a lot better now. His heart rate is back up to normal, doctors say that he will be fine."

"Good. And how is Pooh holding up since she had him?"

"Man … Pooh will be Pooh. She's alright though."

"Cool. Remember if you need me for anything then don't hesitate to ask bro."

"Appreciate it but we're good." He started on his hash browns and sausage.

"We family, we all we got." I announced while digging into my omelet.

"So what's up with you fam?"

"Man … do you know how tiring this shit is?"

"What? Hustlin' or …"

"Trying to have two girlfriends and shit."

"Oh yeah! Been there and done that - that shit ain't no joke especially when you live with one."

"You ain't lying. I can't keep doing this shit."

"That's why I don't get too serious with these girls, too much work involved. And then you could get stuck with a crazy chick - I'm coo."

"Um hum."

"But that chick you brought to the club seemed real cool. Shaun - she fucking hates me."

"Bro, how can you remember anything that night - the way you was all over Lisa!" We laughed.

"That double stack fish was amazing!"

"I know." We laughed again. "But yeah bro, I like Zanada too. She's real coo."

Juan was a tough critic so getting his approval meant something. "Not to change the topic but have you heard from Ricky?"

"About a week ago. I called him yesterday but he didn't answer his phone. He didn't call back either."

"I wonder what's up with him - I'll call him later because I know he ain't up yet. I still trip on the fact that he parted ways from us - there's plenty of money over here for all of us."

"I trip too - don't know why he went out there with those lame ass dudes either."

"We should all hit the club tonight - damn! Not tonight, tomorrow maybe."

"What you got going on tonight?"

I grinned. "Kicking it with my girl."

"Shit which one?"

"You already know."

"Alright now … be-careful messing with those girls hearts."

His words would later make all the sense in the world.

***

The scent was peculiar; a combination of perfumes and oils and different smokes as well. A bar ran along the back wall with a pair of pool tables not too far from the restrooms. The dance floor was in the center with some booths surrounding it and the DJ booth sat in a corner all alone. The music was blaring from distinctive drums and heavy bass lines while the people ranged from all nationalities - Jamaicans, Haitians, Hispanics and Africans all came out to have a good time in one way or another. We caught a feel for the place in a booth that viewed the entire club. The lights were dim but sequenced to every beat and black lights seemed to be a fad. A lot of provocative dancing was going on; slow grinding, fast grinding, some type of full body clap and some of the women were allowing their bodies to vibrate violently.

A short hair lady wearing hip huggers and a Bob Marley t-shirt stopped at our booth. "Ya like ta orda trinks mon?"

I glanced at Zanada in disdain.

"I'm having what he's having." She grinned.

I ordered the usual. "I'm glad that you could understand her because I couldn't."

Four songs later we were on our second round and suddenly a spicy salsa beat took over the club, it was filled with energy! We watched on in amazement as the dance floor filled with couples who were twisting, floating and foot working it. Her whole demeanor changed when she smiled at me.

"I can do that you know - can you dance?"

"Ah … a little bit."

The next thing I knew she was pulling me up by the hand and dragging me to the floor. I had never given a girl so much credit in my life but she … was drop dead gorgeous. Her foreign roots showed heavy; her hair was pulled back into a neat pony tail that was long enough to drape to her mid back as her shirt wrapped around her neck exposing her smooth shoulders and parts of her back. Her lavender skirt hung right below her knees to where her black Manolo boots came to her calf for a perfect match. No words from me as we looked at one another, which should have told her something right then and there. She calmly moved her body to the beat, moved it as if she was born to dance. I played dumb for a split second, looked at her like she had made a mistake but that was until I caught her beat with ease and began to hang with her. Little did she know that I could hang with the advanced class as well. She looked at me in awe when I began to match her moves. We tore the floor apart for at least another song, as long as we had a beat then we were good. We were lost in our own realm when the song was near its end, I elegantly rolled her into me and her dimples gave in, unrolled her back into a light twist, pulled her back with class and grace and like that I allowed her lower back to rest on my forearm. We dipped in style with her right arm wrapped around neck, my free hand gripped her upper thigh just enough to give a few a slight peep show. The beat ended. Her facial told me that she had just had the time of her life. I gave her a quick peck on the lips, she loved the moment. We noticed a few viewers as we made our exit, they began to compliment us:

"Nice sheet, mon."

"That's how you dance!"

"Ay mami papi - I like!"

We were back at the booth when the waitress stopped with another round of drinks:

"Tese are on the house - we like ya dance mon." She pointed to the bar where two other bartenders smiled and waved. We waved back and thanked her simultaneously. She left.

"What were you getting ready to say?" I asked her. But yet another interruption occurred. A pretty Latina stopped in front of us and for some reason she and Zanada resembled. The girl had submissive freak written all over her face. Zanada's eyes nearly popped out of her sockets before she shrieked:

"Carmen!!! Oh my god!!! Your hair - you cut it!" They had a moment while hugging and holding hands. "I haven't seen you since high school - how are you?"

"I'm fine! How are you - oh my god Marcos and I saw you two tear the roof off this place, you guys looked great together!"

I smiled.

"You're still with Marcos?"

"Girl yes - we'll get married one day."

"Carmen I am so rude, this is my boyfriend … Javon. Javon this is Carmen."

I stood and politely shook her soft hand. "Nice to meet you Carmen." I threw my billion dollar smile on but hers was worth a zillion.

"Por supuesto tu gabes como escogerlos, q no es verdad?"

"El es guapisimo!"

She spoke back with a childish giggle "De veras, lo es y sabe cocinar, muy pero muy bien."

I smiled again.

"Well … I'd better get going, Marcos is ready and I've got to get up early in the morning for a million and one reasons but it was so good to see you!"

"I know … we will have to stay in touch this time." They would exchange numbers before hugging and pecking each other on both cheeks.

"Nice to meet you again Javon." She began to walk away.

"Mucho gusto a conocerte." I returned.

She stopped dead in her tracks, turned and glanced at me then Zanada. Her facial said it all.

"Javon! I didn't know that you spoke Spanish!

"Yeah, a little bit." I lied.

"So … you know what she said?"

"That you knew how to pick them and he's fine and then you said yes and he knows how to cook?"

She seemed embarrassed. "And you also knew what I said the first time that we …"

"Hit it harder and don't stop?"

"Oh. My. God. I'm so embarrassed." She shook her head in disgust.

"For what? Don't be embarrassed, it's not a big deal at all."

"Whatever."

"Are you mad?"

"Yes, I am mad." She folded her arms across her chest.

"Why? Because I speak a little Spanish?"

"You know what, it seems to me that all of your "littles" mean the complete opposite. A "little" Spanish, a "little" dancing - seems like all of your littles mean the complete opposite."

"Girl, you're tripping. That's all I know."

She rolled her eyes at me as her diamond earrings winked at me every time a colorful light blinked.

"I guess you're mad … yeap, you're mad. Well guess what? So what, I don't care!" I laughed while stealing a kiss from her. It brought a slight smile out of her precious face. Not a minute later the DJ pumped a Sean Paul and DMX song that started the club back into a frenzy. I pulled her up and back to the dance floor we were. We found ourselves in the midst of having rough sex with our clothes on. *Here comes the boom, here comes the boom.* DMX's voice echoed throughout the air.

We called it a night after two more songs - or so we thought.

CHAPTER 16

"What's up Terri?" I called my sister while pulling onto Keystone Avenue.

"Nothing. Reading. What's up with you?"

"Just left the club. Where is Christopher?"

"Right here sleep. We've been playing all evening - oh and Moma wants some grandkids now."

"I bet she does." We shared a laugh as I passed the message to Zanada. "Okay girl, we will be there first thing in the morning to get him."

"Tell her I said thank you again."

"Tell her I said she's welcome and anytime."

"Bye."

The monitor in the car read 1:02 a.m. and we had just pulled into my complex. The night's chill was in full effect finally and to prove it was a light frost across all the vehicles in the parking lot. We walked in holding one another as the cars on the highway cried in the distance.

The TV was on mute showing videos but was paid no mind. Jay-z was playing in the atmosphere and he was speaking upon all the girls whom he adored.

"So ... is there anything else or any other surprises that I should know about you?"

"What are you talking about - I haven't had any surprises."

"Let's see … you're bi-lingual, you know how to cook, you're great with kids and you can dance - how many guy's do you know who can dance like that?"

I laughed.

"Thank you. I rest my case." Her hands raised up in air for a split second to fall back on her thighs.

"Okay then, what about you? You do a lot of things as well."

"My mother taught me all of the Latin dances before she died and I've spoken Spanish since I was seven - she forced me to." She had a new softer tone.

I should not had said anything to her because I knew that her mother was a tough conversation for her.

"I'm sorry. I shouldn't have … I'm sorry."

"It's okay." Her light smile wasn't enough for me to believe that I was forgiven.

I wrapped my arms around her and pulled her into me. We sat in silence for a while.

"I learned Spanish in school, it was a core for township schools. My grandmother called herself punishing me by putting me in salsa classes when I was fourteen but little did she know that I enjoyed it - well the instructor at least." We laughed. "And the children comes natural I guess."

"What did you get put on punishment for?"

"Uh … borrowed her car."

"She punished you for driving?"

"No, not exactly. I used it to get high in."

She threw the bad boy finger wave at me. "Whatever happened with you and school?"

"I don't know. Got tired of it. I quit during my junior year."

"Your junior year! Wow. Would you consider going to get your GED? Maybe college afterward?"

"I might go to night school for my GED but I doubt college. I think because of that stereotype of college kids, society thinks that if you don't go to college then you're a lost cause. I'm out to prove that wrong. What about you?"

"I'm thinking about it. Thinking about law school."

"Law school! Hell yeah! What kind of attorney?"

"Defense at first."

"Isn't that something, my girl wants to do it big in the world. Wait … can you act? Because that's all an attorney is … an actor who knows the law."

"There's more to it. You are too silly." She laughed.

"I think that you should go for it baby."

She sent me a bashful look.

Silence took over us again. She was probably contemplating on becoming a top-notch attorney while I was pondering on a way to tell Shaun that I needed some space.

"Do you remember when I told my friend at the club that you could cook?"

"Yeah, why?"

"Do you know what that means in the Spanish culture?"

"No, what?"

"It means that if a man can throw down in the kitchen then it is taboo that he gives wonderful sex."

"I knew I had skills for a reason!"

"Mnn hmn, I figured that would blow your head up a bit more." She leaned up to take advantage of my lips. Her lips did it every time, always pushed me over the edge.

I was pinned between her and the couch, she was all over me full throttle. I pulled back from her and stood us up, took her by her hand and led her into my bathroom. I lifted her onto the sink, switched the vanity on and began the kissing again while I straddled in between her. She went for my shirt … I did the same to her but moved my lips to her chest. She positioned herself so I could remove her skirt; seduction could only be described as she sat there in dark cherry Vicky's biting on her bottom lip. I turned the shower on, I undressed, finished undressing her and we got in. I washed her from head to toe; her most sensitive parts first. She returned the favor. Her hand gripped my penis as I watched the water trickle down her chest.

"I want you bad." She whispered.

"You know what to do."

She let go of me and faced the shower head. She'd put me inside of her, found an angle and grinded all over my dick. "Hit it baby." She placed her arms on the wall. Sex faces, wincing and moaning took over us. "Harder. Yes … just like … mnn … yes." She was doing the most. "Se - Se papi - no pares."

"Como asi, mami - ayi mero?"

"Se. Se!"

I stopped suddenly. Raised her leg up to the tub - I plunged inside her and made her rock, roll and jolt. She cried in pure passion as I gripped her waist forcing her into me.

"What are you doing to me … why are … you … doing this to me?"

"Hush girl, no talking." I felt something inside me building. It was on the move.

"I'm … about to …"

I could feel her changing and suddenly I pumped so hard inside her that it felt as if I went past her stomach lining. It happened. Our bodies celebrated together at the same damn time. We slid down to the tub as the water poured on us. Neither one of us could speak, we were out of breath and the celebration had ended. I'd eventually wrap her up in a towel and carry her to my bed but she'd glare at my mirrors that were aligned with the head-board – this is what initiated the next session. We slept for maybe four hours.

CHAPTER 17

I dropped them off around nine the next morning. As I pulled out of her complex I turned my phone back on and it instantly lit up with voice mails. Juan, Terri and Shaun. Something wasn't right.

I called Juan first.

"What's up bro?"

"Man where the fuck you been - I've been trying to find you all night – you didn't answer your door or phone - are you okay - where are you?"

"Whoa slow down man, I'm fine. What's wrong?"

He didn't respond.

"Hello!"

"Uh … bro … Ricky is … dead."

My main organ skipped a beat. "Stop playing like that man."

"I'm serious man. They found him by the abandoned apartments off Raymond Street."

"Who … who found him?" I choked up while running a yellow light.

"Police."

"Shot?"

"Twice in the head. He was in slouched over in the Caddy."

"Got fucking dammit! I told him to leave those south side muthafuckas alone!" I pulled to the side of the road. "This was last night?"

"Yeah. His cousin, Man, the one who he was always with called me and told me. He said he called you too."

"That's all he said?"

"Yeah."

My phone beeped. It was Terri crying and going insane, she repeated what Juan had just told me. It was real, no dream. I went back to Juan. "Where you at? I'm on my way."

We would go to Ricky's moms place.

Every local news channel covered his murder that day. They always found a way to twist the truth up; they said some kids found him in his car with it still running so either the news was incoherent or somebody wasn't telling the full story. What I did know was that Fat Man, his cousin was always beside him since he migrated out south. I wondered why he wasn't with him when he got shot.

I was at home alone. I was thinking, pondering and debating on life. Everyone knew that I was alive and well so I turned my phones off and took some time out for myself. I tried to drink some of the pain away, hell I even tried to smoke some of it away too. Both were flukes.

Juan and I paid for the funeral arrangements and tombstone. We told Ms. Tina to send us every bill possible or whatever she needed but she denied our offers.

In the future I would make it a point to visit his mother. I'd leave money with her that she never accepted.

I would have given every single dollar, car, jewelry and whatever else back to bring him back but that was ignorant thinking. I had no choice but to ponder on the times when we were piss broke and he'd make a way out of no way for us to eat. The days when we young boys running around to Hook's drug store filling our pockets with any and every kind of candy, the days when we had not one care in the world as long as we had our bikes and the days when we evolved into young men had bypassed us far too soon.

I thought way too much after this. Thought that I may had been getting tired of the lifestyle that I lived or was I becoming scared? Fuck no! I was never scared. I may had been shaken up a bit but never scared.

CHAPTER 18

Several days had rolled around and I still hadn't made a move out of my place. I looked a mess and felt trifling. My hair was nappy, beard was living its own life and I probably lost a few pounds that quick.

I received word on Monday that I'd be a pall bearer with Juan and some of Rick's peoples. Ms. Tina wanted me to say a few words but I politely declined. The funeral was held at Grace Hope Baptist that weekend and I wasn't looking forward to it.

I heard a faint tap at my door while I laid on my couch in a serious daze. I ignored it but it grew louder. I knocked an article off the table as I got up to answer the door. Her demeanor read worry and uncertainty: "Hey." She stared at me. "Are you alright … I've been calling you … are you sick?"

I nodded no while allowing her in. She looked like another woman in her work attire. She was highly sophisticated in her gray skirt suit.

"You don't look alright." She placed her purse on the coffee table and sat down.

"I didn't know that you wore glasses."

She ignored me. "What's wrong … you look … rough?"

I ignored her back.

"Helloo …" Her voice raised in a snobbish tone.

I'd glance at her beauty even with worry and disdain she was still a work of art. I had been lying to this girl on a regular basis. Maybe it was time to tell her the truth. Maybe not. She'd be hurt, confused, pissed off and disappointed but at least I'd feel better within myself.

"I'm sorry, what did you say?"

"I said that you look a damn mess - have you eaten, you look hungry?"

"No." I eased towards the bathroom. When I returned she was reading the article.

"Javon, who is this because that last name looks very familiar - do you know him?"

"That's Rick. My brother by another mother."

"What! Oh my God … I'm so sorry baby - I had no idea." She looked on in disbelief. "What happened … who …?"

"Baby I don't know anything. All I know is that he is dead. That's it."

She put the paper down and laid her glasses beside it. She held me like a comforting woman. Someone had raised this young lady correctly. I thought about breaking down for the moment but my strength was being tested. Some men believe that if they cry then they are labeled as *soft* while others thought that *real* men do cry - I had no opinion at this moment.

We laid quiet for quite some time and not once did she remove her arms from around me. I needed her and she was there for me.

"Where's the baby?"

"My father picked him up from daycare."

"What time do you have to pick him up?"

"Whenever but he's fine for now."

"I know your father has to wonder why the hell you always have him babysitting."

"No, not really. He knows that I'm with you a majority of the time."

"Really?"

"He knows all about you, I'm always talking about you and … he wants to meet you." She grinned.

"Ah shit."

"My daddy is cool, he'd love you … trust me."

"If you say so."

She kissed me on my cheek.

"Can you stay with me a little longer?" My emotions got the best of me.

"Baby, I am not going anywhere. I will be right by your side for however long you need me." She meant those words and all I could do was nod my head in shame thanks to my actions. She'd kiss my forehead. "Anything for you … anything. Oh - here!" She raised up to her purse. "These should put a smile on your face." She handed me a Wal-greens photo pamphlet.

I would smile as I flipped through the pictures, we resembled a family - a beautiful family at that.

We sat quiet for a bit longer before I spoke. "He was your doctor's nephew."

"Hunh?"

"Ms. Debra -"

"Oh my god … are you serious! I'll have to send her some flowers or something. Such as damn shame!"

"You know what's crazy … you and I would have never met if it wasn't for Rick because he's the one who called Ms. Debra the night that I got shot." I continued to tell her about the funeral arrangements and how I turned down the chance to speak at it. She would offer her support by attending it with me but I had no choice but to decline.

The funeral came and left. Somehow 'hood funerals always turned into car and fashion shows which was sad but true. People from throughout the city came out to pay their respects. A majority of our 'hood wore black and white hoody's with RIP text and pictures of Rick embedded into them which to me was tacky but a trend that took over urban America. I recognized people from high school, fiends, a few politicians, IPD officers, Phatima and Porsha and the list went on. The boy had so much love in the city that some of the *mom and pop's* businesses shut down during the service hours. His cousin, Fat Man was there but it seemed as if he stayed up in a new females face every ten minutes. He didn't seem to be hurt or upset about the situation at all.

Terri, Mom and Shaun all came but they didn't stay long. I didn't feel like really dealing with Shaun at the time anyways. Ms. Debra and I conversed for a while though. I told her about Zanada in which she found hilarious, she also said that Zanada had a crush on me right then and there that day.

"Such an odd place to meet someone." She chuckled. I did the same.

CHAPTER 19

Two and a half weeks had passed since the funeral and Thanksgiving came like a bat out of hell.

I was back in the streets, not heavy but enough to maintain. Although I had pondered over a possible plan to slow my lifestyle down hopefully by the end of summer.

One of my buddies from grade school was majoring in business at Purdue and when it came to real estate the boy was a genius. He knew his shit when it came to investments, stocks and 401k but anyways he and I were developing a plan, a big plan. And if this plan would work then hopefully I could clean up some of the dirty money within the real estate world and then at this time everybody and their mother wasn't into the real estate game just yet, it wasn't obvious that drug dealers were buying all the section 8 and dollar homes to flip yet.

On Thanksgiving I finally got a dose of being at two places with two different women at once. Shaun begged me to attend dinner with her and her family at her mother's house but prior to that I had invited Zanada to Momas - how did I pull that off? The good thing about Shaun's mother was that her schedule always began early, close to 3pm. My grandmother would usually finish up around 5pm so all I had to do was leave a bit early from Shaun's mothers place.

I didn't eat much at Ms. Rhonda's and then I was fairly rude to Shaun the entire time. I'd play the good guy role around her family but the moment we were alone I'd pick an argument. At first she couldn't understand it but she'd soon tell me that I was emotional due to Ricky. Whatever she saw fit then I rode with it. During the visit I mainly stayed in the back with Shaun's cousin, Tony. He was a pretty boy thug who was a few years older than me but quiet as kept he did his thing in the streets as well. He was very discreet about his business - he almost fooled me but a hustler knows another hustler when he or she sees one. We knew each other's business but wouldn't dare put it out there.

Around 5:30 I said my good byes and thank you's to everyone as they tried to persuade me to stay longer. I kindly told them that I had other family to visit as well. I told Shaun that I was going to visit Ricky's mom in which I knew she would not want to go there with me so I was set.

***

The highway allowed me to open up my new toy and that damn thing drove like the bat mobile! A few weeks after the funeral I traded the Aurora and some cash in for a 2000 black on black Lexus GS 300.

By 6:00 I had Zanada and Christopher in the car with me. She was a bit nervous of course before meeting my family but I promised her that she would be perfectly fine. I felt the same way when I met her father - she was as happy as a fourteen year old boy having sex for the first time while I was as nervous as a catholic preacher at a … never mind. I was nervous as fuck! But everything turned out fine. He had to have been in his mid-forties and sort of resembled a darker version of Cuba Gooding Jr. He was very proper but yet with a bit of "hood" in him. He was well-educated and down to earth as well not to mention that he was a consultant for GM - big money! His miniature library spoke volumes about his knowledge, he owned books such as the *Isis Papers, Life and Times of Marcus Garvey, Catch 22* and *The Trials of Assata Shakur* just to name a few. I didn't know much about those books at that time but indeed I would. He told me that I seemed like an intelligent young man and to keep moving forward. I found a new respect for this man because not only was he a single father who raised a young lady but he was a successful and educated black man in America - last of a dying breed. And so what if he had a thing for foreign women, love is colorless and besides that Latina women are gorgeous as any other woman of any race is. Zanada said that she saw a difference in him since he met a lady from Puerto Rico, they were dating and she was happy to see her father happy.

Momas driveway was packed when we pulled up. As soon as we walked in we were smacked by the aromas of baked turkey, yams and a mixture of Thanksgiving meals. Moma intercepted us in the hallway showering us with hugs and kisses. Christopher giggled away while Moma swooped him up in her arms and left us in the hallway. My grandmother liked Zanada, they vibed rather well the night they babysat Christopher. I put our coats up and took her by the hand to introduce her to the family. They all showed her plenty of love especially my cousin, Sinobia. They acted as if they grew up together. My Cousin Chelsea's son was there with my Uncle Lee which gave Christopher a playmate. Things were going smooth that holiday. Everyone had cocktails that evening except Zanada and I for some odd reason but Moma took the cake; she walked around with a glass of wine the entire night. I didn't know who exactly cooked what but it didn't even matter - the food was amazing! I catered to that girl the entire night seeing if she needed more of anything or less of anything and it was noticed. Uncle Phillip and Aunt Cookie smiled every chance they could at us.

Zanada waited until the entire room was in chatter when she asked me: "Is there any reason why you are the darkest person in your family?"

I told her that I'd been wondering that same question for years and then some. We shared a light laugh. I glanced across the table to witness my sister and her friend smiling at each other and all I could do was nod my head, my baby sister was growing up and there wasn't a damn thing I could do about it. She would be leaving to Michigan State soon - at least she didn't mess up the cycle. My ignorant ass was the only one who did - I guess the black sheep would fuck some shit up. I broke out of my daze when Moma congratulated Zanada on how smart and handsome Christopher was. She thanked her but quickly moma's sisters chimed in to agree.

"You two look so nice together - when are you getting married?" That was my Aunt Tina.

Zanada looked at me then back to Aunt Tina: "I guess when the time is right, and, things seem to be moving in that direction."

My mouth dropped but then another bomb exploded.

"So honey, you two must be in love especially with the affection ya'll share - we see it, he's been catering to you all night." Aunt Shelly had to chime in.

Zanada glared at me although this time with a sparkle in her eye: "Yes, I do love Javon but I think that I have to like him a little more because love changes."

"Oh praise Jesus! I like this young lady!"

"Me too!" That was Tina then Moma.

She won all the women over with that last answer but all the men looked at me like *redeem yourself.*

"Jane look at them … They. Look. Good."

"They sure do! What I want to know is when are ya'll going to have some babies because I need some great grand babies."

"Moma! Ok, thank you … we will kindly let you know." The entire room laughed at me including Zanada. "Someone please take that wine from her!" I protested over the laughter.

An hour or so later we were all lounging in the living room where Will Downing was crooning in the background of chatter, laughter and gossip. The boys were playing their souls out in the toy corner and Sinobia, Zanada and I were relaxing on one of the older love seats where they were discussing that night before hair/fashion show; Studio 22 was the name of it and everyone that was a somebody or at least thought that they were a somebody would be in attendance. Guess I was a nobody because I passed on it that year. I went into deep thought as I admired a picture of my mother, my heart did an odd jump as I reached across to pick it up. My mother had to have been twenty-three and I had to admit that she was gorgeous. I chuckled to myself while comparing my sister and her to one another.

"Is that Terri looking all grown?" Zanada asked.

"No, this is my mother." I said proudly.

She took the picture from me in disbelief. "Oh. My. God. They look like identical twins - they're gorgeous! Are you sure that you weren't adopted?" She whispered loud enough for Sinobia to hear. We laughed. When we were younger Sinobia and Chelsea would get mad at me for only God knew what and they'd taunt me by saying *that's why you was adopted, blacky!*

Eleven o'clock came and the baby was worn out. She didn't want to leave but we had to. We said our goodbyes and thank you's while being overwhelmed with food to go plates. All the men gawked over her when she stood but I couldn't blame them because I would have done the same damn thing. She had the body of a goddess and the appropriate dress that she wore still didn't give her body any justice. As I hugged my Uncle Lee he mouthed the word "nice" to me. I grinned. I was thankful that Moma didn't slip up and call her Shaun's name or anything along those lines because she was tipsy and she says what the hell comes to mind around that time.

We had a real good time that night but … it was a shame that I didn't spend more time with them all. This would catch up with me in the long run.

CHAPTER 20

March 2001

The mid-afternoon temperature had to have been fifty which wasn't bad for mid-march. I was following Juan to an auto detail shop on the south side to have his old school's top repaired.

He pulled into the garage as I pulled into customer parking. I made my way into the shop to check out some audio equipment but four fellas were exiting and one bumped into me. Three of them were fairly tall, dark-skinned and had braids but the fourth was extra light-skinned and had low hair with funny colored eyes - this is who bumped me. They all rocked designer leather jackets with hoodies, jeans and Jordan's - typical thug life gear. Their mouths were filled with gold teeth and they reeked of freshly smoked chronic, strong shit though. I looked back to see them hop into an all-black suburban, I shook it off. I was toying with one of those Kenwood monitors on display as Juan handled his paperwork at the front desk. *Aint no way in hell I'mma pay 1700 for this shit.* I said to myself. Suddenly that scent was right back before me, thought I was alone until I saw two reflections in the monitor. One of the dark-skinned fellas and the light-skinned one, both of their eyes blood-shot red as they pierced into my soul. I became defensive. *Shit! I left my gun in the fucking car.*

"Yo man, didn't mean to startle you but you look real familiar." That was light-skinned.

I noticed that they both wore necklaces with diamond encrusted SS charms which could have stood for two things; super sport or south side.

"I look familiar hunh - well you know how it is … small world playa." I noticed Juan directly behind them now with his hand tucked inside his jacket.

"Aren't you peoples with the brotha who got killed in November out here … Rick, I think?" Light skinned had confusion in his voice.

"Hold up brotha - who are you?" I was calm but more defensive. "And how do you think you know me?"

"They call me Yellaboy and I'm from the projects, Brick city. I was cool with Rick. Thought I recognized you from the funeral but … my apologies homey. Guess it ain't you."

Juan was still behind these brotha's ready for war until I spoke: "Hold up bro, yeah that was me. I'm sure you can understand my defense."

"Most definitely, I understand. But, yeah, Rick was good peoples - I'm sorry for your loss but uh … this is gonna sound crazy and shit but hear me out. Me and the nigga Fat Man is beefin kinda tough, he tried to play me out of some money and … I'll put it to you like this … I got some info for you."

"Straight up … about?" I already knew where this was going. Juan eased up a bit.

"A yo Richard! Let me see a pen real quick." Yellaboy yelled to the mechanic behind the counter. "My nigga, call me around 11 tonight and we will talk then cause this ain't the place nor the time, ya feel me?" He handed me the folded paper then said: "Me and my niggas … we about money, we don't get into that drama unless need be so with that being said you got my word that we ain't have nothing to do with ya man's death."

He tried to assure me. "What you say your name was again?" He extended his hand.

I hesitated but gave my name and shook his hand. They strolled out the store as Juan and I looked at one another.

"You ready?"

"Yeah, let's ride. My shit will be done in several days."

As we hopped in my car we watched the suburban pull out into Michigan street's traffic.

"You think they know who …"

"Yep. Either that or they are on some bullshit."

"You think they did it?"

"Hard to say. But just in case I'm always ready for war."

"Me too." He tapped his shoulder holster that showcased two .45 dessert eagles.

It was just the two of us, we had no choice but to have each other's back. I wouldn't let anything happen to him and he wouldn't let anything happen to me.

***

"What's up?"

"What up, who dis?"

"Javon."

"Oh wassup bro."

"Ready to get down to business."

"Definitely. Where you wanna meet at bro?"

"Let's go for the old church behind the Dome, you know where that is?" It was a fair distance for both of us and if it went down at a church then … so be it. We'd be in the new bible under the book of Exodus.

"Yeah, I know its whereabouts. Give me about thirty minutes, coo?"

"Cool."

We were at the stash house when I made the call but had to stop at the storage to load up a small artillery just in case; .45's, P-89's and a .223 resting along Juan's lap. Had we gotten pulled over that night then we would have either been on breaking news or would have been sent to federal prison that same night.

***

We pulled into the church lot around 11:45 and I immediately saw the suburban with its rear end facing the wall in a dark corner. I killed my lights, backed in next to the truck and noticed that someone sat in the passenger. I nodded and rolled down the window never taking my hand off of my gun.

"What's up bro, check this shit out … I ain't no snitch or nothing but every shady muthafucka has his day right. Well Fat Man is as shady as they come." Yellaboy explained as he exhaled his chronic. He coughed a bit and said: "You wanna hit this my nigga?"

"Nah, I'm good."

"You fam?"

"Nah I'm strait, right on though." Juan denied him. They shot us a look that said we didn't know what we were missing.

"But yeah, me and ya mans was cool but his cousin is a snake. Fat Man robbed one of my stash houses and before that he sold Q here some bad product which all this shit went down prior to Rick coming out this way. I grew up with this dude and even in elementary school he was a snake.

I sat quietly and listened but I couldn't understand where exactly he was going with all of this.

"I heard a rumor a few weeks before the murder about Rick having better product than Fat Man. To make a long story short Fat boy wanted in on the connect and Rick told him no. They had a slight fall out over that shit and a few weeks later Q's little sister found him in his car slouched over the steering wheel." He took a long hit from the herbs, exhaled and coughed.

I thought before I spoke: "So you damn near think that Fat Man - his cousin had something to do with it?"

"With all truthfulness I can't say for sure but … shit don't add up. Let me ask you this, Rick wore a bezzled out pinky ring on his left hand, didn't he?"

I looked over at Juan's pinky finger and nodded my head. We all had those pinky rings, I never wore mine but they did. I remember when we all bought those rings from that cute sister girl at Fifth Avenue Jewelers. "Yeah, he wore one. Why?"

"I saw Fat boy at the club with one on not too long ago. Maybe it was one similar or some shit, I don't know."

The only thing Ricky would sell was narcotics and the only thing he would give away was sex. "Did you hear anything about his jewelry?" I asked Juan.

"No."

I paused and thought for a minute. "Do you know of any spots that Rick had out your way?" I wondered where his belongings where. His cars were at his moms place but where was everything else?

"Nawh, I don't think he had spots out here, not that I know of at least."

Q said something to him in a low tone.

"Oh yeah, he did flaunt this light-skinned chick around; long black hair and a fat ass. She damn near resembled Mya."

"Star." Juan and I said in unison. Star was Ricky's closest thing to a girlfriend. They were on and off so much that they couldn't be labeled as a couple and I hadn't heard from her since the funeral. "What she got to do with anything?"

"Weren't they living together?"

"Sure was." Juan chimed in.

I had no clue. I didn't even know that they had patched their beef up. I was too caught up with my own damn relationships so let alone someone else's. "If I need an address, can you get it?"

He calmly stuck his hand out the window. "I thought you'd never ask."

This was an address that could have decided a man's fate. An address that had no price tag on it … or did it? I reached into my hidden compartment to grab a wad of cash and handed it to Yellaboy.

He took it examined it for a moment and handed it back to me.

"Nawh man, like I said, Rick and I was coo. He was a real nigga. But I'll tell you what … I do need some good shit. We keep getting stuck with that bullshit that's going around, maybe you can plug us with some 100%."

"Oh for sure, we got you on that. You got my number, hit me when you're ready."

"Bet. It'll be in about a day or so." He reached his hand back out. We shook and told one another to be safe. They sped off south as we cruised out north.

CHAPTER 21

Sinobia and Star were pretty close. Don't know how they met exactly but I do know that Sinobia introduced Star and Ricky to each other about a year and a half ago at a bar-b-que that we all went to.

It was late when I called Sinobia, 12:45 a.m. but I needed Stars number ASAP. She gave it to me.

"Hello?" A sexy semi-sleep voice answered.

"Hey Star, what's up … this is Javon. Sorry to wake you but I seriously need to ask you a couple of quick questions.

"Javon … oh my God, how are you? I haven't heard from you since the …" She paused.

"I'm fine. How about you?"

"Making it." She yawned.

"Good, I know it's rough but we will make it through this. But listen, I need to ask you a few questions about Ricky, are you up for it?"

"Sure."

"So you two was living together before this happened?"

"Javon, we've been living together for almost seven months - you didn't know that?"

"I had no clue. Been so caught up in my own drama that I didn't even think to ask."

"Yeah, all of his clothing, shoes and stuff is here."

I thought about extra dope and money but thought twice on it. "Did he leave any money with you or …?"

"We have a joint savings account, it has like 25 thousand in it. But I don't know of any loose cash around here - is that what you're wanting to know?"

"Well yes and no. I'm not looking for money like that but I'm trying to put some things in order to this puzzle. That's all your money, in fact, if you need some more money or anything else do not hesitate to call me. Two more questions and then I'll leave you alone."

"Okay."

"Where is his jewelry?"

"His necklace with his initial charm is right here but he wore the one with the cross the day he was killed and he had on his ring and bracelet too."

"No one has seen or found those pieces?"

"No, not that I know of."

"Ok. And finally, did he ever bring his cousin around over there?"

"The fat one - yes! Fat Man … I couldn't stand him. Just something about him that I didn't like."

"Really? So you didn't trust him?"

"Lord no."

"Ok baby girl, thanks. You have been a huge help but I'm going to let you get back to your beauty rest."

"Okay Javon … be careful out there." She said sincerely before we disconnected the call.

I took a deep breath as I stared at a blinking stop light dead in front of me. My mind seemed to be made up.

"Tonight or tomorrow night?" Juan questioned.

I scratched my head and hesitated. I looked at him and grinned. We switched cars, stopped for gas and cigarellos. We made the journey to the address on the post it.

CHAPTER 22

Our luck and timing was a gift from ... I'd assume the scouting team from Lucifer and Associates. Within an hour of the stake out the brother pulled up exiting his car rather quickly with a pizza box in his hands. Juan put the chronic out, grabbed his .223 as I pulled my glock out. We crept up behind him bare-faced which meant one thing.

"Don't move bro." Juan forced the barrel into his back. "I ain't fucking playing."

I moved in front of him with my gun aimed at his temple. "What's up bro, you good? Here, let me help you with this." I opened the door and asked him "Anybody else in here with you?"

He nodded.

"You sure?" I checked briefly and cautiously.

"Javon, what's this all about?"

I knew he would know who I was from the jump. "Where's your gun big fella?" I patted the 6'0 foot and 290 pound man down to retrieve a chrome .357 long nose from his side. "The fuck you think you are ... Charles Bronson or some damn body." Juan forced him down to the couch as I checked his place further.

"Juan ... my nigga ... what the fuck?" Fear arose in his voice.

"Shut the fuck up." Juan demanded.

I didn't know if Juan saw it or not but I sure the fuck did. The sparkle of it caught my eye. "This is a nice place big fella. Entertainment system is nice, furniture is nice - this marble?" I pointed to a small end table. "Nice low key area out here in Castleton - you doing the damn thang bro." I tried to read his soul briefly but couldn't. "That's a nice ass ring, where can I cop one at?" I moved in to take a better look at it.

He didn't respond.

"Huh? I want one just like that." I stared at him in his eyes as he still didn't respond.

Plop! I smacked him upside his face with the pistol. "Are you deaf suddenly?"

"Ahh!" He yelped as he held his face. "What the fuck is this shit about … I-I-I got it from 5th Ave, got damn!"

"That's all you had to say big fella." I said calmly. "But what if I told you I already have one just the fuck like it?" I raised my hand up to show him my ring. Juan did the same. "Now think carefully as I ask you this next question, did you kill -" I froze in mid-sentence when I noticed something glistening partially tucked in his sweat suit jacket. I approached him closer, gun pointed at his forehead as I gently removed it. The diamonds spoke so many answers. They were so amazing and magnificent the way that they were arranged inside the sign of the holy trinity.

Juan glared at it. My eyes became watery, body turned numb and my mind … my mind was settled on revenge. Revenge was a sin, I remembered that from Sunday school when I was younger - Romans 12:17 or something like that I thought. A sin! Shit! Pre-marital sex, greed, gluttony and numerous other things that I did were sins. I wasn't perfect, no one was. It's life. Was one sin worse than another? I stared into the man's soul once more and prayed. *Dear God please forgive me for all of my sins.* My trigger finger jerked twice. The first bullet probably did it but Juan reached into his holster to remove his .45 and did the same. Two more shots into his chest.

Rest in true peace Ricky.

CHAPTER 23

December 2001

The holidays had come back around out of nowhere and somehow I managed to keep putting Shaun off; it was beyond time that I told her that we should part ways. Each time I told myself I'd do it I'd always back down but this time I had no choice.

I couldn't do the double holidays any longer, couldn't be at two places at once and I couldn't come up with any more lies either. Not to mention that this lifestyle became expensive because as soon as one of them hit me with a guilt trip of never being home or around enough; off to the jewelry store I'd go. I had to play sick on my birthday and valentine's day with Shaun because Zanada had me held hostage for those entire days. Shaun had to of known something but she had me at gunpoint on the 4th of July and spring break which is when we visited Coco beach.

Christmas was near and I loved it. This was my time of the year; loved the snow, the colors, the music but most of all the giving. I loved to give.

I had planned to give Zanada one of her presents early because it required her awareness in advance. I bought us tickets to vacate to the Bahamas in March which I'd give her the tickets over dinner …

"Javon this place is fabulous - look at the view." She was amazed by the high-rise sights of Indy night life. We were at a restaurant that upscale people raved about, Eagles Nest. To me it was all the same.

"Yeah, it's nice."

"How did you find out about this place?"

I was lost for words because Shaun had introduced it to me a while back. "I've been here before."

"Really. With who - another chic?" Her tone came off as jealous but yet interested.

"Would it be better if I plead the fifth?"

"No, because if it was with another bitch then I sure as hell don't have to worry about her because she'll never be back here with you again."

Somehow or another I was turned on by her words. "Yeah, it was with another girl." I tried her.

"That's that bitch's loss, not mine."

"Okay … so how's work going?"

She glared at me in despise before taking a bite of her salad. "Work is … work. Ready for something new but …"

"Like what?"

"Not exactly sure yet but I don't want to work in banking for the rest of my life."

"I think it's time for law school." I sipped my drink.

"It's just not that easy." She sipped her cocktail.

"Law school, bar exam … what else?"

"Time to study, child care, money …"

"It's money not moe - knee. How do you have an accent?"

"I dont, I said money."

"Okay. Anyways, I was telling my grandmother that you wanted to be a lawyer and she tells me about one of her old students; a lady who was black and climbed her way to becoming one of the best defense attorneys in the state. And guess what?"

"What?"

"She had two babies to raise alone during her early stages of becoming one."

Her demeanor read possibility. "Yeah but she might have had some extra money for childcare if they weren't old enough to watch themselves."

"I don't know about that but I'll ask Moma." I had so much faith in this girl. "I think that you should look into some law schools and consider filling an application or two - I'll handle the app fees."

"Let's say that I do fill out an app and somehow get accepted into a school how would I then pay for rent, car note, etc?"

"Good question ..."

"See Javon, you have to think -"

"I don't see why you couldn't come and live with me?" I grinned.

"I'm sorry ... what?"

"Yeah. Pack up and move in with me. If you have to break your lease then I'll pay for it."

"No, I can't - are you serious? First of all I could never be a burden on someone else. I have to take care of my own responsibilities - my child's and my own. And then you only have a one bedroom, we would need another room." With her saying that it seemed as if she was at least considering it. "Oh ... and third, I would hate to mess up your status of having a bachelor pad."

I finished chewing my salad before I replied. "First of all, you wouldn't be a burden. You would be working on bettering you and your career which benefits you and Christopher. And as far as your responsibilities go let me take care of you for a little bit, there is nothing wrong with letting a man take care of his woman, is it? No."

She grinned.

"Besides, when you start raking in all that big money then you can take care of me. Oh and it's no big deal for me to holler at my office manager about upgrading to a two bed or condo - either way it'll work out. Lastly, I guess you broke my virginity from being a bachelor - I was going to have to lose it sooner or later." We shared a laugh.

"Javon baby, I just don't know. I mean this would be a major transformation,"

"Okay, well do this; think about it for a little bit and we will go from there, ok?" Had I lost my mind! I was asking this girl to live with me when I already lived with another one! I needed to go see a doctor because I was acting crazier than crazy.

"Of course, I'll think about it."

"Good." I smiled while reaching into my pocket. "While you think on that maybe you can think on this too." I handed her the travel agency envelope, "Merry Christmas."

"What's this?" She studied the info and mouthed the word Bahamas. Her face suddenly lit up from joy. "What are you trying to do to me - are you serious - I don't know what to say …"

"Yes would be great."

She studied my face, every inch of it for what seemed like hours. "Stand up."

"Hunh?"

"Stand. Up."

As I stood she did the same and walked to me. She gently kissed me on my lips and said: "Yes!"

By then a few couples began to stare and softly clap.

"They must think that -"

"Yep." She smiled her billion dollar smile before sitting back down. "Oh my God - when are we going?"

"Is spring break ok?"

"Of course! I have a lot of vacation time and Daddy will take Chris - will you be able to get off?"

She caught me off guard with that one but luckily I was saved by the bell when the waiter interrupted her question.

"Your dinner will be out shortly and I apologize for the delay." He sat two champagne glasses in front of us before popping a bottle of Dom Perignon.

"I'm sorry sir but we didn't -"

"Oh no sir, it is on the house." He insisted. "Congratulations on your engagement."

She and I snickered lightly possibly like how a couple who had just got engaged would. Dinner came and left and the food and service was great. When the check came she attempted to grab it.

"Uh excuse me but what are you doing?" We began to play tug of war over the bill.

"I'm paying for dinner."

"Thank you but no thank you."

"Javon, let me be a lady. A lady realizes that a healthy relationship consists of fifty fifty from each party - a girl does not realize this."

I released the bill to her while she grinned and pulled her Visa out. I let her pay for dinner that night and I didn't feel bad nor cheap about it. She was right, a healthy relationship consisted of fifty fifty from each party.

***

The next day would have been a day that I finally told the truth for a change. Lying was an addiction; once you start up it just keeps occurring. I built lies around lies - I lied so damn much that I couldn't even remember the truth. But they say that the truth shall set you free … shit! Free from what?

I should have just bought a real one. I was dealing with an artificial Christmas tree that was pissing me off. I heard a car door shut and knew it was her. I helped her in the door with a few bags of groceries. "Hey."

"Hey." She smiled and kissed me.

"How was work?"

"Work was work."

I'd heard that before. I nodded my head in shame.

"How was your day?" She continued to put the refrigerated items up.

"Not bad." I said dryly.

"Um hmn, I bet." She lipped off while heading to the bathroom.

"Shut the fuck up." I thought out loud.

"What you say baby?"

"I said that the sink is fucked up."

She hadn't been home a good five minutes and already she was wrecking my nerves.

"Oh I forgot to tell you that police are everywhere on College."

"Duh. There's a police station on College Shaun."

"If you'd let me finish - not the police station but by your friends variety store. They were in the front and back."

"Who?"

"Your friend who's mixed … Ralphio or Mario?"

"Joolio?"

"Yeah, him. Looked like a bust. A lot of marked and unmarked cars all around his store."

Joolio was twenty-four and he was one of my bigger competitors in my hood if that's what you want to call him. He and I were cool though but mainly on a sociable level. He was born in the Dominican Republic and rumor had it that his mother was raped by a black man from the states which is how he got his nationality. The boy was doing his thing though; he had several stores and a few car washes around the city which all raked in big dollars. The police must of raided his store on 28th and College. I suddenly wondered why none of my youngsters called me with the news. I checked my phone - it was off! I wanted to know more info but she only knew what she saw and my questions to her would only create a feud between us.

"Why all the questions?"

"Just being nosey, that's all."

"Um hmn. Nosey? How about nerves?" She added fuel.

I ignored her as she brought more complaints. She said something about how I never listen to her when it came to the company I kept and some bullshit about me being a fall guy and more shit. I tried to defend myself as she spat a non-ending venom session; she said that I should work for her father at his car lot, how the drug game was only going to lead me to prison or the cemetery and so on. She finally gave up as silence took over us.

Make up sex could have been the best thing ever invented to relieve stress especially if drugs and alcohol weren't around. Round one came before she left to the gym but round two came after her workout so … when was I supposed to tell her that I was in love with another girl? When was I supposed to tell her that we were finished? Before or after she told me that she was pregnant?

I stayed home that night and held her for the first time in a long time. She fell asleep with happiness sketched on her face while mine was drawn with confusion.

The clock glowed in green - 5:01 a.m. I fell back to sleep and awoke again. I couldn't fucking believe it - the wind around clock in my cell read 6:31 a.m.

CHAPTER 24

My soul was on empty and it was scarred. Scarred from all of my dirt especially the dirt that I threw into those girls mouths; more so Zanada.

She was in the court room the day of my sentencing. She sat deep in the back dressed highly professional with shades on. I supposed that she was trying to hide her pain, anger and frustration. I lied to her for only God knew how long and all of it came to the light. She had given me her all and I returned the favor with a black heart.

It was close to feeding time and that punk ass clock read 11 a.m. I didn't feel like doing a damn thing. I wasn't going to no one's mess hall - not that day. I sat in my cell thinking on a million things at once but one of the main ones was why hadn't Shaun brought my daughter to visit me lately and why hadn't I received any mail - *what the fuck!* That was how my next five months went. Pain, bitterness and anger.

It was the third day in March 2003 and I had not heard from Shaun in weeks. I needed to know how my baby was and why she had not brought her to visit. The automated operator did her usual routine and within ten seconds my call was accepted:

"Hello?"

"Hello Javon." Her mother answered.

"Oh hello Ms. Rhonda. How are you?"

"I'm fine honey but the question is how you are?"

"I'm holding up. Taking it one day at a time." In no form or fashion could I show any signs of weakness to this lady because if I did then she would preach to me until Jesus returned.

"Glad to hear that Javon. And you're taking care of yourself?"

"Yes ma'am, thanks for asking."

"Are you staying in your studies - did you receive the Good News bible and bible study charts that I sent to you some time ago?"

"Yes I did, thank you."

"Now you do know that God loves you as His son, don't you?"

I couldn't tell because what father would send their son to prison. "Yes Ma'am, I do."

"Very good. Now I want you to read these scriptures: Lamentations 3. 34-36 and Psalms 91. Read these and the next time we talk we will go contrast and compare our thoughts on what we got from them. Ok?"

"Okay, sounds good."

"Okay baby, I love you and keep your head up and thank you for blessing me with such a beautiful and smart grand baby - here's Shaun."

"Love you too and you're welcome."

"Hey." Shaun said nonchalantly.

"Hey. What's going on?"

"Not much. Getting the baby's dinner ready so mom can feed her."

"Why aren't you feeding her?"

"Because I need to finish getting dressed."

"Dressed? Where you going?"

"I'm going out Javon."

"Oh really … well have fun." I said calmly. "So why haven't you been up here?"

"Because I haven't had any time to. This new job has me extra busy, our daughter is a handful and not to mention how high gas is due to the war."

"Yeah. Yeah. So when will you be up here?"

She hesitated before answering. "I don't know."

My self-control would not allow me to accept anything other than an answer that I wanted to hear. "Don't you think that you should know - you have not been here in weeks - what is the problem?"

"It may be a while Javon."

"A while - the fuck for … Shaun stop making this so difficult."

"How much longer do you expect me to do this?"

"Do what?"

"This prison crap." Her voice raised.

"What do you mean?"

"Javon … I cannot keep doing this, I can't. You need to worry about yourself and figure out how to get out of this situation. You need to - never mind."

"I need to what?"

"I said never mind."

"No say it. You started it so finish it."

"You need to stop being so self-centered, you need to accept responsibility for your own actions and -"

"Alright! I ain't trying to hear that shit - you got me so fucked up right now!"

"No baby, you have yourself fucked up." She whispered. The phone went silent.

"Hello - hello! Stupid ass bit -" I caught myself while slamming the phone down. A couple of the guys on the card table glanced at me as if they knew what I was going through.

She was indeed right. She had been right the entire time. I got myself fucked up.

I received a piece of mail several nights later. It was a piece of mail that I thought I never would receive but maybe it was better if I did not receive it but I'd never know. I began to read it until a $200.00 money order receipt fell out which threw me all the way the fuck off. My thoughts were disturbed by a tap on my cell door. It was M-1

"Wassup bro?"

"Wassup fam. I aint doin' much besides relaxin'"

"Let's go run these bums off the spades table." He pointed to the loud day room.

"Aight coo. Let me read this kite real quick and I'll be out there."

"Aight bro." He'd pull my door to where the noise would lightly fade away.

I started to read the letter:

Dear Javon,

How are you? I can only pray that God gives you strength to get through this trial. I got your information from your sister, I ran into her at Wal-Mart about a month ago and she has really grown into a gorgeous young lady. Anyways, I also got your info off the internet a long time ago but I couldn't put myself through the pain and trouble to write you back then. Javon, I don't know where to begin with this because I'm not much of a writer but I'll try my best. First, let me tell you that your daughter is gorgeous - Terri was holding her in the hallway before your sentencing. And your girlfriend or babymoma whatever she is to you is very pretty too - you sure do know how to pick them. :-) Let me cut to the chase; I'll probably never be able to trust another man as long as I live, you have permanently scarred me not to mention the fact that you already knew about my past relationships. You lied to me about being a liar straight to my face … I trusted you! I trusted you with my life and my son and you know how I feel about him with other men. You and I shared something very special or at least I thought we did. Our mothers, our connection and our beliefs just to name a few. I blame myself as well though. I should not had been so naive and stupid again but … I saw something in you. I saw a man who wanted to be a husband, a loving father, lover and friend all in one. Was that all a front? Are you that much of an actor because if so then you are truly in the wrong business sweetie. I knew something strange was going on by the way you canceled our trip. It's okay though, you are still a good person; I knew you were the moment I first set eyes on you. I'm so sorry how everything ended up because you do not belong there let alone with that amount of time that the judge sentenced you to. That was cruel and harsh punishment especially by this being your first non-violent case ever. They say that everything happens for a reason though.

Javon I also need to tell you something that I had no choice but to do. It was a month and a half after you left when I found out that I was 8 ½ weeks pregnant - I had an abortion. I am so sorry Javon but I had no choice. I couldn't raise another child alone let alone while his/her father was in prison. I couldn't do it again.

I know that I just told you enough to ruin your day, your week or probably even your year but I had to tell you - unlike you I'm an honest person. You'll get through this. I know you will. I pray for your protection and strength every night. Remember that time heals all wounds, keep that in consideration. Take care of yourself oh … and I hope this money can help you out with some commissary.

Always,
Zanada

PS: Theres no need to write me back because I only rented this P.O. box for a few weeks.

My heart began to do something strange after reading it. It skipped several beats followed by a tight gripping pain inside it. I had to drop to my knees, couldn't breathe correctly, couldn't focus. I made a fist and started to pound my chest; my eyes instantly filled with water - what the fuck! Was I having a heart attack, couldn't have been. My breathing eventually came back and the pain gradually decreased. I was able to boost myself up on my metal bunk but I still wasn't feeling right but I maintained.

Four long weeks came to pass since that night and I had absolutely no clue as to what happened. I never had the problem again. I didn't bother with going to the infirmary to get checked out because obviously it was better that I didn't, all the nurse would do is charge me ten dollars to tell me to lay down and take the ibuprofen that she would prescribe. That's all they gave out; a person could be choking and all they would say is "take ibuprofen and lay down" What! Rumor also had it that the medical staff were all improperly trained and had certificates that validated them to be veterinarians at the most. It was best to not go.

I ended up taking heed to Ms. Rhondas request by reading her scriptures. Lamentations 3. 34-36 read T*he Lord knows when our spirits are crushed in prison; He knows when we are denied the rights he gave us; when justice is perverted in court, He knows.*

April 2004

Thirteen more months had gone by after I received another shocking piece of mail that went something like this:

Dear Mr. Hardman;

My name is Dominique J. Williams and I am a defense attorney who specializes in drug and murder cases mainly on a federal level. During my fourteen years in law I have won a total of twelve major trials and lost ten in which six of those were reversed on appeal with that being said I am writing you in regards to possibly representing you on your post-conviction relief which I am sure you are aware that this is your last option on appealing your case before it goes to a time-consuming federal level court. I briefly glanced over your file and records in court #20 and I cannot promise this just yet but it seems as if something foul has occurred during your trial. This cruelty of injustice should open up grounds for a possible retrial and/or perhaps a vacated sentence. In your case I would require a $2000.00 retainer fee and if we progress beyond that point then we shall discuss the balance. If I fail to obtain any relief in your behalf then I will refund half of the retainer fee.

I look forward to hearing from you my brother as soon as possible so we may begin with the necessary preparations for this travesty.

Sincerely,
Dominique J Williams

PS If you were wondering, someone whom prefers to stay anonymous brought your case to my attention.

I had heard something like this before from my first appellate lawyer and that bastard robbed me for $5500.00 - he didn't get a damn thing accomplished. Right after that I spent $1800.00 on another lawyer who claimed that she could get my sentence reduced on a sentence modification - yeah right! She didn't get an hour reduced off my case! That was $7300.00 down the drain and now this guy wanted more money with no certainty on how much more or if he could actually do anything at all. Money did not grow on trees and my money was becoming an issue after lawyers, commissary, my daughter's needs, Terri's wants and my new habit of smoking weed on a regular. I had the two grand that he wanted on my books but the question left was … was it worth it? The man said "brother" to let me know he was black and obviously someone who knew me referred him to me, I thought on this for several days but I went against my better judgement and sent that money to his office at home. Home - hearing or saying that word would make doing time that much harder.

That following week the attorney notified me in regards to receiving the payment and that he had already begun researching my case. We would see where this went.

CHAPTER 25

June 2004

Hot could not define the weather outside. It had to have been at least 90 degrees with no wind whatsoever blowing on this odd day. I was attending college courses; summer school actually - imagine that! Never imagined going to college especially in someone's damn prison but at least I kept the family cycle in motion. Going to school kept me occupied a majority of the day and time didn't seem to drag like how it did before, it also beat sitting in a cell doing nothing all day.

The counselor, Ms. Van Roy notified me that morning about coming to see her before going to class but there was already a line outside her door. I'd have to see her after class, but, only if that was not probably another one of the biggest mistakes of my life. Now quiet as kept if the opportunity ever presented itself I would have fucked the shit out of Ms. Van Roy! She was basically the average white girl with ocean blue eyes, huge tits and a booty that probably needed to get hit from the back a few times in order to inflate it. But then again, if an inmate was to get caught fucking around with any member of the staff then you were liable to get murdered in which I witnessed one time before during my stay. So you always had to think twice about that.

On the yard I couldn't seem to get 50 cents "Many Men" out of my head but I made it to class.

10:50 came and class was finished. While headed back to my housing unit I noticed that the yard was packed; looked like two recreation lines were going at once and then with school letting out the area was jam-packed. Saw my homey M-1 standing next to Black Mike and a gang of the fellas from our hometown on one of the ball courts but directly across from them on the other side look like a mob of GI fellas (Gary, IN) all watching the 3 on 3 battle on the court. I showed M-1 some love and said what's up to a few other brothers. I viewed the game as well and shook my head in disgust because prison ball was a tad bit different; ego's flared, fouls were extinct and it was a shame that you couldn't wear protective padding because those boys played dirty as fuck. The vibe didn't seem right from the start. An F-18 roared above us in the clear blue sky, nothing new since the air-force base was connected to the prison.

"What's going on bro?"

"Seems as if the GI niggas had some words with Black Mike's cousin." M-1 answered quietly to me.

This wasn't anything new with the Gary brothers and this was a reason why I stayed to myself, I couldn't afford to fight another man's senseless battle. A lot of the men in prison rolled in groups rather it be city with city, religious, homosexuals, aryans or whatever - people stayed with who they fit in with. But on this day the heat, ego's, animosity and doing time did not mix well one bit at all - maybe if the president would have used this concoction for a weapon for the war in Iraq then just maybe he would have seen better results. GI dudes moved closer towards us; all dark-skinned and over 5'11 with bulk to them. They actually all resembled but … so the fuck what!

"A yo, what the fuck you looking at bitch ass nigga!" That came from the smallest fella in our bunch and that just about did it because within seconds I was in the middle of a war zone.

"Fuck it." I thought. I got all damn day anyways, I wasn't getting out of prison anytime soon so why not go have some fun. The devil took over me once again in my life which he had a great way of doing. The devil had me mentally, physically and emotionally when I was out in the world so why not in prison! Every single man fought for what they thought was right except myself. I knew better. The same way that I knew better about all of the shit I had been doing; I knew a million other ways to earn legit money, the same way I dogged both of those girls, and the same way I knew that I had no business taking another man's life - I knew right from wrong. I squared up with a baby face brother who had fear soiled into his eyes which could be the worse ones because a young boy who was scared were as dangerous as they came. We brawled for at least sixty seconds trading forceful blows but with no blood drawn just yet. The boy had heart and a descent right hook but my upper cuts were too aggressive for him. We were in a zone until a parade of whistles blew, correctional officers by the dozens were sprinting our way and some wore riot gear armed with tasers, mace and rubber bullet shotguns. The military base would soon be on standby. I made a huge mistake by turning my head to measure their distance but I was suddenly jabbed in my chest. He then went for my chin but missed as I bucked to my knees, my heart skipped a strong beat again and again. The kid ran off. I could not breathe once again - deja vu. I felt light-headed and slowly my body began to shut down. No air to breathe but all I could hear was "Get down you fucking niggers, get the fuck down!" Two c.o.'s stood in front of me and one of them was trigger happy the other enjoyed spraying mace.

"Get. The. Fuck. Down!" He pulled the trigger - great aim. He hit me dead in my chest. I fell straight to the ground even with the free throw line. I pounded on my chest trying my best to rebuke the pain but it felt as if my heart was trying to leave my body by then. A ring started to ding in my head as the c.o. maced me heavily and snatched my arms forcefully behind my back to cuff me. I pleaded to him in a low whisper: "I-I can't breathe man … I can't breathe."

"What? You can't breathe, is that what you said boa?" The voice reminded me of one of the brothers from the Dukes of Hazard. "Well so fuckin what boa -" Blah … blah. I was being speared in the head by his butt end of the shotgun. "Can you breathe now boa, hunh?"

At that point I could no longer feel any other pain besides the first, it overruled. I must had been getting beat pretty bad because I could faintly hear M-1 yelling "Come beat me like that punk bitches!"

But those would be the last words that I remembered hearing that day. My body was numb and all I could see was gray and black fussiness that soon became pitch black.

"What's that noise?" I thought. The sound of med-evil horns took over; the kind that was heard when royalty was in the coming - loud but mighty.

"What is this? What … pictures?" Pictures were floating right before my eyes; my precious daughter passed by, Ricky was laughing in his, I was lying in a bed soaked in blood but then my grandmother and mother smiling and hugging each other flew by. My sister, Shaun then Zanada sitting together and there I was again; I was young and dressed in a suit holding a dollar bill in my hand. The picture show ended. A bright beam of light blurred my vision as more horns blew. "What is that?" Something flew past me. A dove. A dove flew past from out of the darkness and into the light. Something said to follow it. I did. I followed the dove to the point where I saw no more darkness.

EPILOGUE

Eventually the guards dragged Javon to the infirmary but of course it was too late. He was Life Lined to the main hospital in Kokomo where he was pronounced dead. The autopsy revealed that he had an enlarged aortic root, his heart was literally too big. His heart began to leak over a lengthy time frame and eventually it exploded which explained his irregular heartbeats, chest pains and loss of breath. The blows to his chest, the impact of the rubber bullet and stress only aggravated the illness. It could have been prevented by him having a surgery but of course he had no clue that he even had such an issue.

His family had issues with the department of corrections releasing his body due to political reasons and the bruising on his body that could not be explained. All things done in the dark must come to the light because his family filed a wrongful death suit against the doc and won a significant amount but no money would bring Javon back.

Suppose that Javon left the ball court early that day and went on his way back to his housing unit to speak with his counselor, there is a strong possibility that he could have been at home as we speak. The counselor held a piece of legal mail that would have changed his destiny. His lawyer had the privilege to send him the tremendous news of his case being vacated to illegal police procedures in which his trial attorney should have argued this issue pending his trial. It's amazing what being at the wrong place at the wrong time can do in life.

Mrs. Hardman donated to several heart research centers after the passing of her grandson. She wanted to prevent as many heart illnesses that she could. She grieved for quite some time but her God calmed her soul by letting her know that her favorite grandson and only daughter were together again with Him.

Terri, his sister, decided to transfer from Michigan St to Indiana University not only to be back close to her grandmother to grieve but to fulfill her dream as a journalist.

LaShaun took the loss of her child's father very bad especially after the way she had cut him off from seeing his baby. But she and the baby moved out of her mother's house into a spacious home in Carmel, IN. She never knew of Zanadas existence.

Juan had the audacity to show up at the funeral but was quickly denied entrance, LaShaun was not allowing that and she caused a huge scene. He fell completely off his square after testifying against his right hand man.

Zanada took his death very rough as well. She visits his grave site faithfully, usually on Sundays. December 17th fell on a chilly Sunday with nothing but gloom and depression in the forecast however it was also her son's birthday which is also the first time Javon and her met.

Hey Javon. I miss you so much that it physically hurts. This is worse than a horrible nightmare. I told myself that I would not cry this time but I can't help it. Christopher always asks about you and for the death of me I couldn't find the right words to tell him that you're gone, he loved you! And I will always love you! I am so sorry for not visiting you while you were in that place, I was just so hurt that I hated you then you would have never understood but then again you understood everything about me. I still dwell on that choice when I had the abortion … I'm so fucking sorry - I should not had done that! And when I found that your case was going to be overturned I planned on telling you this face to face, and another thing baby; the lawyer who helped you was my father's eldest brother - my uncle. I wanted you out of there so bad that I told him about you, prison wasn't a place for you but I wonder if I had went to him sooner than … ok I'll stop. I do have some great news! I took your advice - I'm going to law school in Atlanta next year! Thanks to your grandmother, she's even paying for a nanny for Christopher. She said that it's what you would have wanted for me and I agreed. Thank you so much Javon. You and I shared something that no man will ever replace in my life and I mean that. I have to move forward but there will not be a day that you are not in my heart, only time will heal this wound. I love you my prince.

As she walked away something unique occurred; the rays from the hiding sun broke from nowhere accompanied by Mother Nature's white tears. Her bouquet became covered in snow as it rested on his grave. This was his favorite time of the year.

ACKNOWLEDGMENTS

First and foremost, I must thank God for all of my blessings, trials and tribulations – past and future. They have all helped build me for a better me in some type of form or fashion. My Grandmother and Mother, thank you for all of your love, support and for molding me into the man that I am today – I love you both to no limits. Aunt Kay, none of this would have happened without you, I remember you staying on me asking "Are you done yet? Hurry up!" Lol! I love you and Uncle Harry to the moon! To ALL of my extended family across the country, I love you all!

Big Robin, Aunt Jackie, Shatha, Barbara, Kenny, Kisha, Angela, Keyiona, Keana, Derron, Porschea, India, Luther, Brian, Mahogany, Ed and Tony; THANK YOU ALL for holding me down in one way or another during one of the darkest times of my life! Sometimes when you go through a situation you seriously find out who your truest family and friends are. Tone, Lomax (LNO), Chirell, Nate, Ja-mil, Pede, Tyrone and to all the other amazing people who read my manuscript when it had sour cream & onion chip grease stains on it. Ha! Thank you for pushing me forward with what I thought was nothing. Ray, Leon, Bernie, Ronnie, Eddie, Barry, Pupe, Terry, Ron

C, Josa, DJDJ and to all my fella's who have shown me love throughout life's journey. To all the men and women who are incarcerated, never give up on fighting your case! Fight the system till its back is blown out! Do not succumb to the definition of "institutionalization" and all I can ask is that when you get home then try a more legitimate route, it will work just believe in yourself. Keep your head held high by all means.

To Fred, Kevin, Miranda, Mike, Joey and Gina; may you all Rest In Heaven.

Shout out to all the wonderful people in the world who don't judge books by their covers and to the people who believe in second chances. Sometimes in life that's all a person needs, a chance.

As I was writing this story I debated on how far I'd go with it. I did not want to write another typical "hood" novel which is why I tried to water down the "illegitimate" activities as much as possible and stay along the path of relationships even though they were not exactly faithful ones. There have been numerous cuts from the original because of my growth and maturity but I believe there is a part of this story that each and every single one of us can relate to. With that being said… this is a work of fiction and none of the characters are real. Ha! I wonder how many of you beg to differ.

If I forgot to mention you then please forgive me. These acknowledgements are from 2006 – I'll get everyone on the next novel. I promise!

Peace and love.
Jon Chris

Printed in the United States
By Bookmasters